I0632361

Annie Chambers Ketchum

Christmas carillons, and other poems

Annie Chambers Ketchum

Christmas carillons, and other poems

ISBN/EAN: 9783741193927

Manufactured in Europe, USA, Canada, Australia, Japa

Cover: Foto ©Andreas Hilbeck / pixelio.de

Manufactured and distributed by brebook publishing software
(www.brebook.com)

Annie Chambers Ketchum

Christmas carillons, and other poems

A. Chambers-Ketchum.

CONTENTS.

L'ENVOI.

MEN give their best to them they love the best;
   The sceptre to the queen, the laurel-wreath
   To the rapt minstrel, and the jeweled sheath
To him whose sword has stood the battle's test.
What guerdon, then, for thee? what garland blest,
   What mightiest wand and blade and tempered shield?
   I bring thee arms by fiercest proof annealed;
I bring thee flowers nor blight nor storm may wrest.
When on thy heart, triumphant from the hells
   Of childbirth-pain, Love's first flower thou didst bear,
     The miracle of this dower thy soul didst prove.
O deathless joy, which motherhood foretells!
   Take, then, my child, as Life's divinest share,
     Thy sceptre, crown, and shield, a mother's love.

From Harper's Magazine.

THE ANNUNCIATION.

Copyright, 1880, by Harper & Brothers.

Page 1.

CHRISTMAS CARILLONS.

TWELVE CHIMES—CHRISTMAS TO TWELFTH-NIGHT.

I. THE ANNUNCIATION.

"ALL-HAIL!"
The angel greets the Virgin mild:
"Hail, Mary, full of grace! thy Child
The Son of God shall be."
Ring out o'er land and sea
        Glad bells, All-hail!
Immanuel comes to you and me.
        O Babe new-born
        This happy morn,
        O Flower from thorn,
            "All-hail"
We sing, with radiant Gabriel,
Hail, Mother of Immanuel!

II. THE SALUTATION.

"All-hail!"
The Virgin bids Elizabeth;

And at the magic of her breath
The unborn Baptist leaps to greet
The unborn Christ he comes to meet.
  "My soul
Doth magnify the Lord!"
Repeat the gracious word
  From pole to pole;
Magnificat with Mary sing,
Hail, Key of David, hail, our King!
  Ring, happy bell,
Thrice hail to our Immanuel!

III. THE NATIVITY : HOMAGE OF THE BEASTS.

  Noël!
"My soul and life, stand up and see
Who lies in yonder crib of tree."
  Bal-loo-la-lo!
  Ye happy bells, ring low,
The ox, the ass, the lamb, adore
This child upon a stable floor.
  Bal-loo-la-lo!
  O happy bells, ring low,

And with the kneeling cattle say
The holy *Benedicite.*
Noël! Noël!

God with us, our Immanuel!

IV. THE HOMAGE OF THE SHEPHERDS.

Noël!

The shepherds see the angel bright
Who sings to them at dead of night;
They leave the sleeping flock,
And follow on, with joyful feet,
To see the Child, the Mother sweet,
The manger in the rock.
Noël! Noël!

Adeste with the shepherds sing,
Venite adoremus ring.
Noël! Noël!

All-hail to our Immanuel!

V. THE HOMAGE OF THE THREE KINGS.

Noël!

The skies the wondrous story tell;
The Orient kings afar

Obey the herald star;
They bring their gifts to Jesu's shrine:
   Melchior, the gold to crown Him king;
Jasper, the priestly incense fine;
   Balthasar, myrrh for suffering.
King, Priest, Redeemer! Ring, each holy bell,
Sing with the kings of Orient and the star,
      Noël! Noël!
All-hail to our Immanuel!

VI. THE HOMAGE OF THE ANGELIC CHOIRS.

    Noël!
The captains of the cohorts nine
Come down to lead the song divine;
"Glory to God in highest heaven,
And peace on earth to men be given!"
   Ring out, and never cease,
     O happy bell,
And with the angels sing the Song of Peace.
   The *Gloria in excelsis* ring,
   Hosanna to the new-born King!
    Noël! Noël!
  He brings us peace, Immanuel!

From Harper's Magazine.

Copyright, 1880, by Harper & Brothers.

"THE SHEPHERDS SEE THE ANGEL BRIGHT."

Page 3.

VII. THE WARDER'S CRY OF GOOD-WILL.

Noël!
Good-will toward men! Ye warders four,
 Go, call, with brazen horn,
Thief, robber, magdalen, outcast poor,
 This happy morn;
" A-yule! a-yule!" send forth the girth
To all the corners of the earth;
"The city gates wide open be;
Come in! Immanuel sets you free!"
  Ring, holy bell,
  A-yule! Noël!
He brings good-will, Immanuel!

VIII. HOUSE-DECKING.

Noël!
Bar out the master from the school;
Mirth comes with peace. Bring in the yule.
 Ye lads and lasses, go,
 Fetch ivy, holly, mistletoe,
  For hall and mews;
  If Jock refuse,

Then steal his Sunday breeches, Kate,
And nail them to the gate.
Noël! Noël!
Sing, lads and lasses, sing Noël!
He brings us mirth, Immanuel!

IX. THE WASSAIL-BOWL.

Was-haile!
Sire Christmas brings the wreathèd cup
With apples, ale, and spice filled up.
Was-haile!
Each ancient grief and grudge we drown;
The Lamb's-wool smooths the roughest frown;
Drink-haile!
Peal, merry bells, peal out apace,
We pledge Immanuel's day of grace—
Was-haile! Noël!
He brings us joy, Immanuel!

X. THE BOAR'S HEAD.

Was-haile!
Bring in, upon his silver tray,
With minstrelsie,

The boar's head, armed with garlands gay
    And rosemarie ;
The lemon in his tuskèd mo',
He laughs amain, " Noël!" I trow.
      Was-haile !
Be gay, ye lordlings, more or less,
The boar's head leads the Christmas mess.
      Was-haile! Noël!
    Give thanks to our Immanuel !

XI. THE CHRISTMAS-PIE.

      Was-haile !
Bring next the meats with mickle pride ;
The plover and the partridge pied,
Woodcock and heron fine,
Good drink thereto, the Gascon wine ;
      Was-haile !
And then, whiles pipe and tabor ply,
The best of all, the shridded pie.
      Drink-haile !
Without the door let Sorrow lie !
      And gif she die,
We'll shroud her in the Christmas-pie.

Was-haile! Noël!
He brings good cheer, Immanuel!

XII. TWELFTH-NIGHT: CHOOSING KING AND QUEEN.

Was-haile!
Your places, lads and lasses, take,
To find your fortune in the cake.
Was-haile!
Jock gets the bean,
And chooses Kate for queen.
Drink-haile!
Now foot it in the reel,
Each frolic heel;
Ye maskers, that a-mumming go,
Stay yet, and point the toe;
" Bounce, buckram, velvets dear,
For Christmas comes but once a year!"
Was-haile! Drink-haile! Noël!
Good-night! Sleep well!
God keep us all, Immanuel!

DOLORES.

DOLORES.

In beauty fairer far
Than the divinest dream of him who drew
The stately Eos guiding up the blue
 Apollo's golden car—

From the dusk realm of Night
Comes forth the radiant Morning, brushing back
The clouds, like blossoms, from her rosy track
 With diamond dews bedight.

The priestly mocking-bird
Wakens the grosbeak with his early hymn;
And down the slopes and through the woodlands dim
 Sweet, holy sounds are heard.

Her gold-enamelled bells
The tall campanula rings. Midst daisies white

The lithe, slim phalaris [1] flaunts his pennons bright
    O'er all the grassy swells.

    Benzòin's breath divine
Spices the air; the jasmine censers swing;
Among the ferns beside the darkling spring
    The mailed nasturtions shine.

    The brown bees come and go;
His cheerful tune the lonely cricket sings;
While the quick dragon-fly, on lightning wings,
    Darts flashing to and fro.

    Pomegranates golden-brown
Drop delicate nectar through each rifted rind,
And ghostly witch's-feather [2] on the wind
    Comes slowly riding down.

    The gray cicada sings
Drowsily midst th' acacia's feathery leaves;
Around her web the caterpillar weaves
    The last white silken rings.

---

[1] The ribbon-grasses (*Phalaris Americana*) along the shores of the Gulf of Mexico are remarkable for their splendid colours.

[2] The down of a species of thistle.

September silently
His pleasant work fulfils with busy hands;
While, cheering him, floats o'er the shining sands
　　The murmur of the sea.

Deep in the shady dell
The cowherd, whistling at his own rude will,
Lists, with bared head, as from the distant hill
　　Rings out Saint Michael's bell—

Calling, with warning lips,
Matron and maid, albeit the south-winds blow,
To climb the height and pray for them that go
　　Down to the sea in ships.

The fishers in the boats,
Mending their nets with murmurous song and noise,
Stop sudden, as Dolores' silver voice
　　From the gray chapel floats:

They think how, o'er the bay,
The sailor bridegroom, from her white arms torn,
Sailed in the haze and gold of Michaelmas morn
　　One year ago to-day;

Then, rocking with the tide,
They reckon up the news of yesterday,
And count what time to-day, within the bay,
    The home-bound ship may ride.

    Dreaming, the long night hours,
Of white sails coming o'er the tossing deep,
At dawn Dolores from her strange, glad sleep,
    Arose to gather flowers:

    Cups honeyed to the brim,
And fruits, and brilliant grasses, and the stems
Of myrtles, with their waxen diadems
    To offer unto him.

    Beside the chapel porch,
The Gloria ended, lingering now she turns
To look, as on the brightening spire-cross burns
    The morning's golden torch;

    Then sees, with sober glee,
The swift, prophetic sea-gulls flying south,
Far out beyond the landlocked harbour's mouth,
    Into the open sea.

From Harper's Magazine.　　　　　　　　Copyright, 1871, by Harper & Brothers.

"'STEADY, THOU FRESHENING BREEZE,'
HER DARK EYES SAY."　　　　　　　　　*Page* 15.

" Steady, thou freshening breeze,"
Her dark eyes say, as o'er the sparkling main
She gazes—" steady, till thou bring again
    The ship from distant seas ;

" So, ere his golden wine
The setting sun adown the valley pour,
Dear eyes may watch with me, beside the door,
    The autumn day decline."

O breeze, O sea-birds white !
Ye may not bring her, from that rocky coast,
The stranded ship, nor wrest the tempest-tost
    From the black billow's might !

But when she wearily
Shall pray for comfort, of that country tell
Where all the lost are crowned with asphodel,
    And there is no more sea.

SEMPER FIDELIS.

SEMPER FIDELIS.

SHE stands alone, on the rose-wreathed porch,
   Gazing, with star-like eyes,
On the white moon lighting a silver torch
   In the glowing western skies;
While her cheeks and her tresses kindle and scorch
   In the sunset's fiery dyes.

Her broad straw hat with its loosened bands
   Falls from her shoulders down;
Idly she frees her slender hands
   From their garden-gauntlets brown,
And smiles, as she smooths her hair's bright strands,
   And looks toward the distant town.

High overhead, 'round the tower's bright vane,
   The circling swallows swoop;
Tinkling along the bowery lane
   The loitering cattle troop

To drink with the snow-white yonquapéne [1]
　Where Babylon willows droop.

Black as jet, in the sunset's gold,
　Loom spire and buttressed wall ;
Soft as a veil, o'er the tangled wold,
　The twilight shadows fall,
While the white mists rise from the valley cold
　And climb to the mountains tall.

Now bounding out to the rustic stile,
　Now crouching at her feet,
Her setter's bright eyes wait the while
　Till hers shall bid him fleet
Down the dim forest's scented aisle
　With wild-wood odours sweet.

Of what is she thinking while her hand
　Caresses the fond old hound
Fidelio, whelped in Switzerland
　And trained on Tuscan ground,
His throat still wearing a golden band
　By kingly fingers bound ?

[1] The familiar name—derived by the Spaniards from the Indians—for the beautiful lotos-flowers so common to the lakes and lagoons in all tropical regions of the Western world.

Semper fidelis : on the clasp
   The glittering legend shines,
As when the giver linked the hasp
   'Neath Conca d'Oro's vines,
Then, silent, sailed where torrents rasp
   The pine-girt Apennines.

She hears again Saint Rosalie's bell
   From Pelegrino's height;
Ave the fishers' voices swell
   Across the waters bright;
While incense-like from the Golden Shell
   Rose-odours bless the night.

From Posilippo's poet-shrine,
   Haunted by flower and bee,
She sees the peaks of Capri shine
   On the rim of the sparkling sea;
She sings 'neath Ischia's fig and vine,
   She dreams in Pompeii.

Where soft Venezia's mellow bells
   Float o'er the silver tide;
Where bright Callirhöe's diamond wells
   Deck dry Ilissus' side,

Or where down the sandy Syrian dells
　　The wild, scarfed Bedouins ride;

Bright as in those long-parted days
　　Fair classic scene and song
In all their magical, phantom grace
　　Back to her memory throng;
Yet framing ever one thoughtful face
　　Their arabesque among.

Swallow and tower and tree forgot,
　　She spans the chasm of years;
She talks with him, by shrine and grot,
　　Of human hopes and fears;
Of lives spent nobly, without a blot,
　　Of blots washed clean by tears.

Brilliant and proud that dazzling train
　　In the classic lands so fair;
Pilgrims gay from the sparkling Seine
　　And the cliffs of Finisterre;
The Austrian pale, and the fair-haired Dane,
　　And the Kentish lady rare:

Yet he turned away with sober grace
　　From each haughty, titled hand,
And sought the light of a charming face
　　From the distant sunlit strand
Where a tamarind-shaded river lays
　　Its floors of golden sand.

Title nor diadem was hers;
　　Yet—true to truth, O fame!—
No record in history's graven years
　　E'er roused a readier claim
To the good man's love, or the coward's fears,
　　Than her simple Saxon name.

So, dowered with her own pure womanhood,
　　Regal in soul as in air,
Where coronets flashed with their ruby flood
　　And crowns with their diamonds rare,
Ever a queen among queens she stood
　　Crowned in her braided hair.

Yet ever, albeit with trembling lips,
　　One answer, o'er and o'er,
While her bright eyes suffered a strange eclipse,

She gave to the vows he bore:
Troth plighted afar, where the wild surf drips
  Down the cliffs of a Southern shore.

What though she felt, with a keen despair,
  She had grown from that childish vow;
That the plodder who won it, though earnest, bare
  No trace of her likeness now;
That the wreath soon to gleam on her chestnut hair
  `Would circle an aching brow?

What though he urged that the demon Pride
  And the tyrants Chance and Youth
Forge chains that forever should be defied
  For the deathless spirit's ruth;
That a false creed's logic should be denied
  For the majesty of truth?

Silent, she showed him the quaint old ring
  On her twisted chatelaine—
A soldier's gift from a grateful king—
  With its legend's lesson plain,
To be worn, whatever the soul might wring,
  Bravely, without a stain.

Shine on her softly, white moon, to-night!
　Thou, only thou, dost know
How she kept—true child of the belted knight
　Who won it long ago—
That ring's stern *Semper fidelis* bright
　And clean as the Jura snow.

Softly !　Thou heardst the deep sea break
　At the foot of the terrace sward,
When she said—while the words of their doom she
　　　spake—
　No fate need be reckoned hard,
Since duty, well done for duty's sake,
　Is ever its own reward.

Softly !　Next morn thy wraith in the skies
　Looked down on a wraith as pale,
Transfixed and deaf to Fidelio's cries
　As he ramped on the terrace rail
And bayed the sea, where his mistress' eyes
　Followed a fading sail.

Kingdoms have risen and fallen since then ;
　Prelate and prince have found
　　3

Both altar and throne the scoff of men,
  And glory's dazzling round
Summed up, to one thoughtful spirit's ken,
  In the life of a silken hound:

One spirit on field and council-floor
  Of first and best repute;
Spotless amidst the strife and roar
  Of mad Ambition's suit,
Still finding the worm at the bitter core
  Of kingcraft's golden fruit;

And pausing midst victory's din, perchance,
  Or the hazard game of power,
To dream of a sea where the sunbeams dance
  And the white clouds sail or lower;
To call up a woman's tender glance,
  And a bitter parting hour.

While she who turned from a throne away
  In steadfast, royal truth—
Stemming the tide she might not stay,
  For duty as for ruth—
Hath wrought in a miracle, day by day,
  The promise of her youth;

Till the one for whom she gave up the ways
  Of a life with high hopes fraught,
And chose a place with the commonplace,
  The spell of her spirit caught,
And the lustrous gold of a noble grace
  With his coarser fibre wrought.

Bright with all eloquent, potent things
  This home of quiet peace;
Ebon and palm from the desert's springs,
  With the marble gods of Greece;
Conch and coral and painted wings
  Of birds from Indian seas;

Helmet and shield in the frescoed hall,
  Bronzes beside the door,
Clefts where the cool, clear waters fall,
  Waves on the lonely shore,
Blossom and cloud and mountain, all
  Teaching their sacred lore.

Sweet from the gnarled black ebony wood
  Flowers the fragrant snow;
Pure from their rocky solitude
  The singing fountains flow;

Fair 'neath the chisel sharp and rude
   The living marbles grow :

So blessings begot of the wakening morn
   And the peace of midnight skies,
Feature and form and voice adorn
   And shine in her amber eyes,
Aglow with the deathless beauty born
   Of stern self-sacrifice.

Shine on her softly, as she stands
   To catch the signal light
From a father who waits beside the sands
   To see, o'er the waters bright,
A ship sail in from the classic lands
   With a gallant child to-night.

A sudden gleam through the alleys green ;
   Fidelio flies apace ;
Glad voices float on the air serene,
   And then, the fond embrace
Of a boy with his father's quiet mien
   And his mother's radiant face.

They sit 'neath the crystal chandelier
   And list, with smiling eyes,

As he talks of the Alpine yodel clear,
   Of the pifferari's cries,
Of the lazy song of the gondolier,
   Of Hellas' golden skies;

Then, sad, of the carnage in fair Moselle;
   Of his school-fellows scattered wide,
When the convent was shattered by shot and shell,
   Its portals wrenched aside,
Where Saxon and Frank who fought and fell
   Were gathered side by side.

Then one and another strange romance
   Of the battle's ruthless test;
And last, the tale of a princely lance
   With the death-wound on his breast,
Clasping close, with a star-like glance,
   A portrait beneath his vest.

"No one its history could trace;
   None knew it, except the dead.
One of our priests—who had served his race—
   The night before we fled
Gave me the picture, because the face
   Was so like mine," he said.

A gold-framed portrait with vermeil dyes:
   A woman, standing pale,
In the glow of soft Sicilian skies;
   And a hound on a terrace rail
Baying the sea, where his mistress' eyes
   Follow a fading sail.

————

They have sung with the boy a welcome back;
   They have chanted the evening psalm;
The swallows sleep in the turret black,
   The winds in the desert palm;
Silence broods o'er the bay's bright track,
   And the mountains cold and calm.

The spicy breath of the deepening night
   Floats through the oriel fair,
As the moon looks in with her parting light
   And rests with her silver rare
Beneath the bust of a mail-clad knight
   On a woman bowed in prayer.

LA NOTTÉ.

Out of the many contradictory stories concerning Antonio Allegri da Correggio, historical critics have sifted the facts that he lived, unknown and comparatively poor, during the tumultuous opening of the sixteenth century, when the midland cities of the Romagna suffered most from the strifes of the Bianchi and Neri begun centuries before; that his wife, Girolama Merlini, was the model for his finest pictures and the lode-star of his life; and that just as he was about to set off for Rome, through the influence of Giulio Romano, he died suddenly of fever at the age of five-and-thirty.

Golden the light on Parma's stately fanes;
And spicy-sweet the spring-time's early breath
Borne northward from the terraced Apennines,
O'er blossoming vines and snowy orchard flowers,
And broidered meadows sloping to the Po.

Golden the light; yet brighter still the eyes
Of a pale dreamer with uplifted face,
Lingering a moment on the strada broad—
Where stands the mighty angel's statue tall—

Then passing, silent, through Saint Michael's gate,
While yet the angelus vibrates to the noon.

What though his cheek with fever's subtle flush
Is hectic, and the way before him long?
His heart is stouter than his beechen staff;
Cheered by a friendlier wine than that distilled
From fair Romagna's grapes-of-paradise.[1]

He sees the silvery river's twisted streams
Netted with flowery islands.   On yon slope
Young children play with kids; and, whistling low,
The lithe-limbed, sinewy mulitieri drive
Their laden beasts along th' Emilian Way.

The triple crown, the lilied oriflamme,
The haughty standard of imperial Charles,
Flaunting its proud *Plus Ultra* to the sun,
The trumpet's boisterous blare, the flashing lance,
The glittering casque, are past, as in a dream.

War's turbulent clangour silences no more
The wild birds in their coverts.   Peaceful stand
The sentinel poplars in their gold-green plumes

---

[1] *Uva paradisa*, the fine yellow grapes of the Romagna.

Beside the Enzo bridge where late the hoofs
Of flying squadrons scoured th' affrighted land.

The soft cloud-shadows chase each other now
O'er violet gardens ; barefoot, laughing boys
Plash in the brook ; beneath her cottage porch
A white-coifed woman stands with levelled hand
Shading her dark eyes from the westering sun.

All greet him as he passes.   By the stile
The grandsire gray looks up and blesses him ;
The low-voiced mother lifts her prattling babe
And prompts its sweet *buon giorno ;* in the fields
The vintners doff their tall caps from afar.

Then to each other, one by one, they talk
Of that grand Easter morning, when, midst wreaths
Of incense, while the organ's thunders rolled,
They knelt in Parma's Duomo, every eye
Fixed on the pictured dome then first unveiled.

A miracle !   No painted roof is there,
But this blue sky of Italy, these clouds
Curled by the south-wind, where with cherub wings
The little ones they dandle on their knees
Bear the white Virgin through the quickening air.

The saints wear household features.   There they see
The grandsire in Saint Peter glorified ;
While he, the grandsire gray, he kneels apart,
And sees, through tears, despite her new-made grave,
His daughter, in Our Lady's radiant form.

The day declines.   On yonder sunny bank
Beyond the Crostolo for a while he rests,
The patient, worn Allegri, all his face
Kindling with benediction as he looks
Toward far-off Mantua's faint horizon line.

Not all in vain, throughout the battling strife
Of Guelph and Ghibelline has he broke the bread
Of sorrow, trusting the prophetic voice
Within him—*keeping*, earnest year by year,
Faith with himself, prime duty, seldom wrought !

To him, th' unsought, th' unseeking, there have come
No fine court favours.   He has never seen
Lorenzo's gardens nor the Vatican ;
Parma, Bologna, Modena, Mantua, these
Inscribe the limits of his narrow world.

Narrow yet boundless.   Morning unto him
Unlocks her gates of pearl.   The wizard Noon

Tells him deep secrets.   Sunset, purple-robed,
Leads him through halls of chrysolite and gold,
And Midnight spins her silver in his dreams.

The shadows lengthen, yet, entranced, he sees
Only the visioned future as he rests ;
Mindful no longer of the broken faith,
The grudging spite, the cruel scoff and taunt
Of recreant churchmen,[1] scornful of his worth.

" Not all in vain," he muses—" not in vain.
But yesterday Romano came and went,
The brave, frank Giulio, with his noble words
Calling the freshness of my boyhood back.
Good angels guard thee, Mantua, for his sake !

Giulio, by prince and cardinal sent, and bearing
A message from the mighty Florentine.
Girolama mia!   We will go to Rome,
And the great Angelo shall see from whence
La Notté's and Saint Catherine's grace are caught.

---

[1] The ecclesiastics of Parma refused for a long time to pay Correggio
for his work in the cathedral, calling its splendidly foreshortened figures
un guazzetto di rane—a hash of frogs.

Chaste mother of my boys ! Whose wisdom rare,
Eclipsing even thy beauty, through these years
Of toil and trust my guiding star has been,
Well might Romano say I owe to thee
The brighter fortune dawning on us now."

And she—all day within her quiet home,
In fair Correggio, she has thought of him ;
Counting the busy hours till his return ;
Pondering the wondrous message Giulio brought,
And singing at her work sweet, thankful hymns.

'Tis late. She goes to meet him at the spring,
Pomponio laughing gaily by her side,
Her baby at her breast. The brook is crossed,
The hill-path climbed. She sees him lying still
Under the fig-trees, in the reddening light.

She kneels beside him, hushing reverently
Her children's prattle as she brushes back
The tangled meshes of his nut-brown hair :
"So tired, so tired ! O patient, steady heart,
Sleep yet a little, while we watch thy rest."

Slowly his dark eyes open at her touch.
The sunset for a moment gilds her hair,

Her children shine transfigured. Still he lies,
Smiling with fixed, calm gaze, while darker grow
The shadows as he feasts upon her face.

O sky, whose lazuli ceiling roofs the world,
Brood with your tenderest grace of mist and star;
O Earth, whose motherly bosom holds us all,
Pour your most precious balsams as she bends
To catch his last low whisper—"Not in vain!"

It hangs there on the wall, Correggio's *Night*
Copied by thee, thou of the glorious soul
And dauntless spirit! All my lonely nights
Are brighter for its presence—may my life
Be better for the lesson it has taught!

PALLAS-ATHENA.

PALLAS-ATHENA.

C. C.

THE sages tell us genius is the fruit
Of centuries.   One child alone came forth
From Scio's golden cycles.   With blind eyes
Turned from without, he tracked the world of thought,
Counted its fabulous shapes, and gave to men
That beautiful religion which has made
Classic and consecrate each Tuscan flower,
Each Greek and Roman stream.

                    One prince alone,
Prophet and seer, sprang from the lusty womb
Of Europe's last millennium.   With bright eyes
Gleaming like opals, from each bog and fen
Goblin and witch he summoned ; from the air
Fantastic sprites ; and from the human heart
Its hidden skeletons, its demons fierce,
Or, with a seraph's high authority,

4

Its godlike virtues and its graces fair.
Swift as the lightning, over land and sea
His subtle witchery sped.   The little child
Looking for buttercups, the grandam gray
Mending her winter fire, the cow-boy blithe
Babbled his wit, not knowing whence it came;
And they whose polished, sensitive ear had caught
The magic of his verse, sought far and wide·
In eager hope that from the lifeless page
Some spirit weird as his might call to life
The wondrous shapes he pictured.

                              Hope had died
Or dwindled to the meagre stunted thought
That the grand visions of the English seer
Were but ideal children, when at length
From Avon's Jupiter, armed *cap-a-pie*,
Thou, goddess-queen, didst spring.

                            We see thee tread
Macbeth's still midnight chamber, and the shapes
That haunt our own deep hearts start up, and point
Malignant fingers at us.   'Tis not thou
We gaze at till our spirits shake with fear,
But dark Alecto, born anew of blood.

Scene after scene beneath thy magic wand
The Stratford wizard's peopled world unfolds.
We laugh with Rosalind; we descant with Jacques;
Bright Portia's wit and wisdom play at will
Before our senses; gallant Henry woos
Fair Katharine and most fair; Ophelia comes
Bedight with rue and pansies; white-haired Lear
Distracted sobs, *Cordelia, stay a little!*
And Juliet sings *Ten thousand times good-night.*

We look again, as o'er the enchanted stage
Thy proud cothurnus treads.   We see the calm
And stately child of Ferdinand, whose firm
Castilian courage awes our ready tears
Back to congealment.   Breathlessly we note
The queenly, sad appeal; the haughty tone;
The lofty bearing, the majestic woe;
Till, at the last, we start to find us here,
Dwellers in modern time, and from the leash
Our fettered pulses freeing, while the blood
Leaps through each trembling artery, we feel
That life's Erinnys dire in thee become
Eumenides indeed.

                    Others have trod
The Shakespeare world before thee.   Some have wept

Like Juliet and Ophelia; some have died
Like Katharine, some have plotted like Macbeth,
Or jested like gay Rosalind in the wood;
But thou alone hast conjured, with thy spell,
All the enchanter's fancies into shape
And made them speak at will, from grave to gay
From lively to severe.

                    We are most proud
To say thou art American, but this
Is meagre claim for thee.   Unto no land
Nor line dost thou belong; thou shin'st eterne
In the fair parthenon of mimetic lore,
Pallas-Athena, helmeted and throned.

From Harper's Magazine.

Copyright, 1871, by Harper & Brothers.

"THE FISHERS IN THE BOATS,
MENDING THEIR NETS WITH MURMUROUS SONG AND NOISE." *Page* 13.

AUBADE.

Awake, m'amie!
The dawn is up, and like a red flower blows;
The gray-beard sea
Smooths all his wrinkles out, and laughs and glows.
Bloom, then, for these and me,
Sweet rose;
Awake, m'amie!

Arise, m'amie!
The field-flowers smile on all their butterflies;
The humble-bee
A wandering minstrel sings, the cricket cries;
Smile, then, on these and me,
Dear eyes;
Arise, m'amie!

Make haste, m'amie!
The rude day comes full gallop.   Let us taste

With flower and bee
The joy of youth and morning; O make haste!
No time have those or we
To waste;
Make haste, m'amie!

BROTHER ANTONIO.

THE wood-yard fires flare over the deck,
As the steamer is moored to a sunken wreck.

They glare on the smoke-stacks, tall and black;
They flush on the quick steam's flying rack;

But shimmer soft on the curly hair
Of children crouched by the gangway and stair,

And rest like hands on the furrowed brow
Of an old man bent o'er his shrouded frau.

Dark sweeps the restless river's tide,
While the pall of night comes down to hide

From the careless gaze of strangers near,
The pale thin form on the pine-plank bier.

They had come from the legend-haunted Rhine
To the grand New World where the free stars shine,

Seeking the fortune they might not find
In the Fatherland they had left behind;

And while the proud fleet ship would toss
The spray from her wings like an albatross,

Their shouting children sung with glee
Wild, stirring songs of the brave and free.

They saw the Indian isles of palm;
The Mexique shores with their spice and balm;

And the Mississippi, an inland main,
With its orange-groves and its fields of cane.

Sweet, round the tawny river's mouth,
Blew the rare odours of the South,

And bright in the reeds, as the steamer sped,
The white crane gleamed, and the ibis red.

But the mother's blinding tears would fall
As she thought of her own loved Rosenthal;

Of the bubbling spring by the minster gray,
Of the vesper-hymn at the close of day;

Of the yew-tree's shadows, soft and dun,
On the grave of Benno, her first-born son;

And while the fever, sure though slow,
Quickened her life-blood's ebb and flow,

She saw, in the sunset, the hills on fire;
She heard, in her dreams, the bells of Speyer;

She talked of the chapel-master's child,
Brown-eyed Greta, so gentle and mild,

Who played with Benno beside the door
And sang with him in the minster *Chor*,

And loved him best till the stranger came
And lured her away with his eyes of flame.

So, ere they reached the far-off goal
Where boundless prairie gardens roll

From river to mount in their flowery braid
Like play-grounds by the Titans made;
3

While all her little ones 'round her crept
And looked in her dying face and wept—

She closed her sunken, faded eyes
Forever on alien woods and skies.

They were far from consecrated ground,
And the unshorn forest before them frowned;

But a vagrant footfall would not press
The lone grave in the wilderness;

So, turning away from his cherished dead,
With a quivering lip old Hermann said,

As he looked toward the peaceful, virgin sod,
"I'll bury her there, in the name of God."

They dug her grave in the forest lone,
While the night-wind murmured a sobbing moan,

And the wood-yard fires, now red, now dim,
Peopled the dark with spectres grim.

Then laying her in her lonesome bed,
Though no funereal rites were read,

He buried her where the wild deer trod,
With a broken prayer in the name of God.

Captain and crew to the boat go back
With the motherless, wailing children—alack!

The rousters [1] work, but they do not sing
As the light pine-wood on board they bring.

The old man kneels in the sacred place;
On the cold damp clay he lays his face;

When out from the gloom of a moss-hung tree,
A low voice murmurs, "Pray for me."

He sees in the thicket a dark-browed man
Where the green palmetto spreads its fan;

His tall form hid in the darkening night,
His face aglow in the flambeau's light.

A moment more, and a palm-branch fair
Is laid on the fresh-heaped hillock there;

---

[1] Rousters, or roustabouts, the negro deck-hands on the Lower Mississippi steamers. Their wild songs, as they work, are well known to all Southern *voyageurs.*

The stranger kneels by the silent dead—
"I, too, have buried my life," he said.

"*Kyrie eleison!*"   Low and faint
Old Hermann utters the Church's plaint.

"*Christe eleison!*"   The stranger's moan
Thrills the air with its rich, deep tone.

The boat-bell rings ere the prayers are o'er:
The stranger looks toward the wave-washed shore,

Then passes away from the flaring light,
Saying, " You've saved a soul to-night!"

The old man sits, while his children sleep
On their steerage pallets, his watch to keep.

Over his head, in the cabin gay,
The glasses ring and the gamesters play.

They talk of Baden and Monaco bright;
They sing, they jest, through the livelong night;

Then, yawning, they ask, as they plan and plot,
Why the chief of their *partie* joins them not.

And he—they reck not he is afar,
Watched alone by the morning star.

Still he stands in that lonely place,
Seeing only the pallid face

Of one who has haunted him East and West,
Dead, with a dead babe on her breast—

Outcast, for his sake, from all below,
Yet chaste, he knows, as the mountain-snow.

———————

Fair in the morning's rosy fire
Saint Lazarus lifts its silver spire.

The river circles the garden 'round,
And the still, bird-haunted burying-ground.

Children about the cloisters play,
And tell, as a tale of yesterday,

How the corner-stone by the bishop was laid,
And Brother Antonio a deacon made—

Brother Antonio, 'round whose head
The brown bees hum when the hives are fed;

Who pulls the weeds from the garden-walks
And shields from the sun the tender stalks;

In whose boat the fisher's children ride
And sing as he rows to the farther side;

About whose feet each helpless thing
May buzz and blossom and crawl and sing—

Brother Antonio, who gave his gold
To build this home for the sick and old;

Who teaches the lads in the village class;
Who helps old Hermann mow the grass,

Or sits at his door in the twilight dim,
And sings with his sons their mother's hymn.

The ships come in with their emigrant poor
Crowded like sheep on the steerage-floor;

But smiles on the lips of the feeblest play
As Brother Antonio leads the way,

Guiding their babes with a tender care
Down the noisy deck and the gangway-stair

To the hospital grounds so fresh and cool
Where the gold-fish glance in the sparkling pool,

And the gentle Sisters day and night
Watch by the sick on their couches white.

Many a nook in the graveyard fair
Is bright with lilies and roses rare;

But one wild spot by the river-side
Is fairest at midnight's solemn tide;

And there, where the green palmetto's fan
Shadows a headstone gray and wan,

Where the long moss swings and the eddies moan,
Brother Antonio prays, alone.

A TREATY OF ELD.

5

A TREATY OF ELD.

No zephyr played among the terebinths
That shaded Bethel's side. The silvery boughs
Of the gray olive-trees that climbed the height,
The feathery cassia's lithe and pliant stems,
Even the aspen-leaves, hung motionless
In the red sunset. The voluptuous breath
Of orange-odours freighted the still air;
The faithful benzoin, clinging to the rocks,
From leaf and flower distilled its incense fine;
The camphire's spicy clusters gave their sweets;
But no light-wingèd convoy came to waft
The benison of fragrance down the slopes
To the fair camp of Abraham, where, beneath
A snow-white tent wrought cunningly with gold
Shone Sarah's wondrous beauty, rivalling quite
The single mellow star that smiled upon her
From the clear eastern sky whose crystal roof
Arched the tall palms of Häi.

Falling dews
Baptized the lowly hyssop; and the goats
Homeward returning brushed its last late flowers
And on their silken fleeces bore the faint
And precious odour past the patriarch's door.
From out her low black tent, barbaric tricked
In cloth of crimson woollen, dark-browed Hagar—
The gift of haughty Pharaoh unto Sarah—
Came, dusky as the night that fell around her,
Bearing a jasper vase of spikenard, sealed
With Egypt's royal signet.   Pacing slow,
Her yellow mantle falling prone apart
From her smooth shoulders, idly now she watched
The distant camp of Lot; now, curious heard
The mellow twitter of the twilight birds;
Till, pausing underneath the clustering vine
Draping the branches of an oak that sheltered
Her mistress' broidered covert, she unloosed
The sandals from her brown and slender feet,
And, passing on unshod, stood silently
Where the pomegranate with its scarlet flowers
O'erarched the purple curtain of the tent;
Then, lifting from the vase its silver lid,
She scattered to the air its priceless breath.
Reverent came Eliezer of Damascus,

And kneeling with averted face before
The curtained opening where Sarah's robe
Of finest needle-work fell delicate
Over her jewelled sandals and athwart
The silken couch that held her comely limbs,
Swung from a golden censer grateful fumes
Of cinnamon and calamus and myrrh.
But naught could tempt the stagnant air to yield
Even unto her, so fair to look upon,
The courted balm of freshness, sweeter far
Than costliest gums.

           Westward, across a glen
Where smiling waters late had sung between
The patriarch's camp and Lot's, dark sullen groups
Stood midst their weary herds just driven in
From thankless pastures. No benignant cloud
Since the new moon at Abib had bestowed
Its blessing, and the raging Lion[1] now
Leading the sun, brought fiery Thammuz in.

---

[1] The critical reader will remember that, following the familiar law governing the precession of the equinoxes, the sun, in the time of Abraham, entered the constellation *Leo* at the beginning of summer—the Jewish Thammuz answering to a part of June and July.

Broad meadows, smiling in the early rains,
Now parched beneath the sevenfold glowing heat
Gave store no longer even to the ass.
The mandrakes failed. No pleasant hum of bees
Prophetic sung of honey in the rocks.
The purple figs were gathered long ago ;
Not until Elul, the pomegranate's globes
Would yield their amber nectar, nor the grapes ;
And these were meagre food for hungry men.
The corn from Egypt dwindled in the sacks,
And the bare olive-trees no promise gave
Of goodly oil to buy renewed supplies
From Pharaoh's granaries even should plenty reign
Until Marchesvan. Morning after morn
The ruthless Canaanite had dogged their flocks ;
Day after day the crafty Perizzite
Hid in some thicket, stealthily had sent
His barbèd arrow to the timid throat
Of kid or lambkin ; while the swarthy men
Who tended Abraham's cattle tauntingly
Boasted of Egypt.

　　　　　　Gloomily the thoughts
Of the proud Syrian herdsmen backward went
To Padan-Aram with its friendly tribes

Of pastoral people; with its corn and wine;
Its goodly rivers and its mellow fruits;
And bitterly, as down the rocky bed
Of the dried streamlet the onagra shy
Essayed to find some pool to slake her thirst,
They eyed the herds of Abraham gathered fair
Upon the eastern slope. There quiet stood
The camels, patient both of thirst and heat,
Cropping the juicy locusts from the boughs
No humbler beast might reach. There Pharaoh's kine,
A princely gift, contented chewed the cud
Of barley, by the cunning cow-herd stolen
From the fast-failing stores. There, fiery-eyed,
Tossing his silken mane and whinnying low
Beneath the almond-trees, the desert horse
Ate the sweet lentils from his keeper's hand;
While the Egyptian, with triumphant glance
Scoffing the Syrian, stroked each shining flank
And laughed derision back.

              The shadows dun
Gathered on peak and palm; and one by one,
The hosts of heaven in silent majesty
Came forth and lent their glory to the night.
At Bethel's shadowy foot, erect and firm,

Grasping his almond staff, the patriarch old
Stood with his face toward Salem.   In the west
The young moon, fast declining, reverently
Silvered his white hair with her parting beams;
Astarte,[1] holding out her golden sheaf,
Named unto him, as with an audible voice,
The gods his fathers served beyond the flood;
While red Arcturus, wheeling on his course,
Mocked him with treachery to the stately faith
That reared the walls of Nineveh, and decked
With marvellous symbols the embattled towers
And palaces of Babylon.   He had turned
His back on proud Assyria with her grand
And opulent cities, at the word of God;
With Lot, his well-beloved, leading forth
Women and men and cattle, he had left
The flowery plains of Haran and the grave
Of Terah; he had passed the brazen gates
Of fair Damascus; never looking back,
He had come out into this wilderness
Not knowing whither, only seeing still
By faith's clear eye the city with foundations,
Whose builder and whose maker is the Lord.
Wandering from Sichem and the plain of Moréh

[1] The constellation *Virgo* was worshipped as Astarte by the Phœnicians.

In search of greener pastures, Famine sore,
Tracking their footsteps like the evening wolf,
Drave them to Egypt.   There, abundant grain
Gave for a season to their murmuring men
The rod and staff of hope ; but once again
Gaunt Famine glared aloof from hill and plain,
And cheerful hearts, erst following lightly on
Wherever he had led, now sullen sunk,
Weary with hope deferred.

                       Night came apace.
Behind him in the tents the lights went out,
Leaving the camps in darkness to essay
The fitful sleep of discontent ; yet still
Stood Abraham, looking toward the holy hill
Where dwelt Melchisedek, the King of Peace.
One after one the chambers of the south
Hung out their golden lamps o'er Salem's towers ;
And drinking in the knowledge of the night
Till Dagon,' sinking low toward Sidon's sea,
Foretold the morning watch, he scarce had heard
The heavy tread of Lot who, sleepless, came,
Preventing the cock-crowing, to rehearse

---

¹ We are told that the beautiful star Fomalhaut, in *Piscis Australis*,
was adored as Dagon by the Phœnicians.

With dark, tempestuous brow, the angry strife
Begun already in the wakening tents.

Abraham remembered Ur—Ur of the Chaldees.
There, midst their fathers' honoured sepulchres,
His brother Haran lay.   Lot, Haran's child,
Fatherless from a babe, had grown beside him
Unto the dignity of man's estate.
Together they had learned the wondrous lore
Of Mazzaroth from the Chaldean seers;
Together from the towers of Nineveh
Had watched Orion's glittering bands, and talked
With burning hearts of him whose sign they were,
Nimrod the mighty hunter.   They had stood
By Terah's tomb in Haran's pleasant land;
And firmly side by side with girded loins
Together they had left their heritage
Obedient to God's mandate.   Had they come
Into this desert only to be filled
With bitterness?

They stood beside the stone
Where Abraham built an altar to the Lord,
When first they came from Sichem.   Silently
They watched the enkindling lustre of the night,

Till the sweet influence of the Pleiades
Softly the golden day-spring ushered in.
Then, with mild accent:

                          "Let there be no strife,
I pray thee, between thee and me, nor between
Thy herdmen and my herdmen," Abraham said,
" For we be brethren.   Is not the whole land
Before thee ?   Separate thyself, I pray thee,
From me.   If thou wilt take the left hand, then
I will go to the right ; or if thou depart
To the right hand, then I will go to the left."

Lot lifted up his eyes.   The morning light
Crowned with its topaz fire the stately line
Of river-palms that eastward stretched away
Toward Zoar.   There lay Jordan's fruitful shores
Well watered everywhere, even as it were
The garden of the Lord ; there cities proud,
Vying with Babylon, lifted to the clouds
Their haughty turrets.   Then Lot chose him all
The plain of Jordan ; and while yet the dew
Decked with its diamonds the blue hyssop-flowers

That grew beside the altar; while the dove
Hid in her lonely cleft on Bethel's side
Still sung her morning psalm, in heavenly love
They parted, each to his allotted way,
Separate, yet knit in holy brotherhood.

A story for all time.   No Mine and Thine
Drew the sharp sword of fratricide; no taunt,
Keener than steel, drove with its venomed point,
That deadlier shaft which rankles in the soul
Beyond the cure of drugs.   Though history write
The same dark chronicle from Cain to Christ,
From Salamis to Sedan, 'tis sooth to list
Sometimes to legends friendlier: to dream
Of Mispeh's pillar, built on Gilead's slope;
Of Penuel's daybreak, when, the blessing won,
While yet the shadowy morning-dusk required
No sunrise save the golden light that shone
'Round the departing angel, Esau came
And standing where the rippling Jabbok sung
Its silver tune beneath the olives, gave
The kiss of peace to Jacob: sooth to know
That there have been, and so shall always be,
Virtue and Truth to silence Vice and Shame;

And spirits ready even midst battle's din
To catch the deathless hymn—

                "How beautiful
Upon the mountains are the feet of them
That bring glad tidings and that publish peace."

LAZARUS.

LAZARUS.

THE morning shone upon Judea's range
Of rifted marble as a pilgrim pale,
Journeying from Bethabara, the rough
And gloomy gorges traversed with a band
Of earnest followers.   Behind them frowned
The baffled wilderness where vultures preyed
And hungry tigers crouched.   The angered peaks
Pointed malignant shadows after him
Like the defiant fingers of a foe;
But on before him, bordering the plain
Of Jericho, serene and flowery slopes
Knelt down to do him homage.   The light wind
That dallied with the fragrant terebinth
Or sung to the green fig-tree and the plane
A careless roundelay, in reverence now
Hushed its gay melody, and, whispering low
Among the listening almond-trees, brought down

6

An offering of white blossoms to his feet.
The brooks that wandered from the northern hills
Seeking the hallowed Jordan, silently
Floated past barley-fields, or in the shade
Of ancient olives murmured as in prayer;
While, on their fringèd borders, hyacinths
Offered sweet incense from their azure urns,
And 'neath the plumy palm-trees galbanum
Sent up its spicy, consecrated breath;
For he who passed was Christ.

               With steady tread
He walked toward Bethany, while earnestly
Unto each other His disciples talked
Of the poor widow and her son, of Nain;
And hushed their tones to whispers, as they spake
Of the great blessing He was soon to give
The stricken sisters. On His brow divine
Gathered the beaded sweat of weariness,
Yet He pressed firmly on, nor paused for rest
Within the valley skirting Bethany
Until the triune height of Olivet
Cast a rebuking shadow toward the fierce
And frowning Wilderness, as if to say,
"Get thee behind me, Satan!"

From the gates
Came forth a frantic mourner.   Her long hair,
Blacker than Egypt's night-plague, heavy hung
About her shoulders, and a flood of tears,
Bitter and salt as Dead Sea water, scathed
Her olive cheek, whose dark tint darker grew
Beneath the evening shadows and the cloud
Of her o'erwhelming grief.   The outstretched hand
Of the Anointed clasping, in a tone
Wild as the wail of Galilee when winds
Dash the black waves on rocky Gadara
And the gray tombs give echo—

"Lord," she said,
"Hadst thou been here, my brother had not died."
Turning away then bitterly, her frame
Shook like a tall young cedar lashed by storms.

"I am the Resurrection and the Life."
Clear as the seraph-tones that spake from heaven
To Hagar in the wilderness, those words
Like a deep organ's modulations fell
Upon the silent air, while the bared heads
Of the disciples bent in reverence low.
Gently and long He spake ; and as the dew

Descends on Hermon's blossoms, on her heart
He poured the blessed balm of tenderness,
Till the grieved maiden's lithe and rocking form
Straightened in holy strength.   Then looking up
Calm as the lofty Lebanon when storms
Have passed away, and the unclouded sky
Kisses its lifted forehead, she replied,
"Yea, Lord, I do believe;" and with a step
Firm as the patient camel's, bearing on
Its burthen great and wearisome, she turned
To go for Mary.

            When the cock crew shrill
In the dim, waning night-watch, and the moon,
Leading the morning, with her silver sword
Parted the clouds and robed the Olive Mount
With light as with a garment, Martha came
With Mary and their kindred.   O'er the eyes
Of her meek sister, that had ever worn
The upturned look which makes us think of heaven,
The white lids drooped, as in the dewy night
The pale convolvulus closes.   The deep folds
Of her blue mantle o'er her slender feet
Trailed heavily, and her slight fingers pressed
The veil of linen on her marble brow

With a pained, weary movement, as she went
To meet her Lord.   She knelt and kissed IIis feet,
Those sinless feet she erst had bathed with tears ;
And casting back her veil, while the bright waves
Rippling and golden of her loosened hair
Swept o'er His dusty sandals, from her lips
Came the low murmur—

              " Lord, hadst thou been here
My brother had not died."

                Then silent there,
She waited for His blessing.

                 Jesus wept—
Wept, though He knew their grief would soon be
      changed
Into rejoicing at His gracious word ;
Wept, though He knew His heavenly hands, ere long,
Within their darkened homestead would again
Establish and relight the inverted torch.
O ye who see along life's sterile paths
The wretched and bereft, ye may not bring
Back to the parched fields of their barren life
IIope's radiant spring-time, nor the holy dews
Of love and trust; but can ye not extend
The one, last solace, kindly sympathy ?

" Where have ye laid him ? "

" Master, come and see."

They neared the sepulchre.   It was a cave,
And a stone lay upon it.   " Take away
The stone," He said, and lifting high His hands
He prayed aloud.   With grave, inquiring looks
In earnest reverence now the faithful ones
Who journeyed with Him gazed into His face.
Like the aurora and the dusky night
Waiting the resurrection of the morn
The sisters watched the open, silent tomb ;
And when the sun above the grizzly peaks
Of the dread Wilderness a victor rose,
And, crowning the calm slopes of Olivet,
Made a bright shimmer on the raven hair
Of Martha, and among the golden curls
Of Mary like a trembling halo lay,
Jesus cried :

" Lazarus, come forth ! "

His voice
Like the quick influence of the opening spring
Unlocked the life-streams death had frozen quite ;

And as the sunrise looked into the grave,
He that was dead came forth, bound hand and foot.

" Loose him and let him go," the Master said.

From hands and feet they draw the linen bands,
The white sudarium from the brow and chin.

" What hast thou seen, O Lazarus ? " we ask
In this mad age the child of prying Doubt,
The mother of Despair—" what hast thou seen ? "

Not so those gentle Sisters in their joy ;
Not so the chosen Twelve ; they question not :
They are content to see the dead alive.

And he, the newly risen, in silence stands,
His forehead pallid from the awful shade,
His eyes aglow from the eternal light—
Content to wait till Christ, who oped the tomb,
Shall ope the sealèd lips, and bid the tongue
Rehearse the strange, unutterable song.

Yet still we clamor: " Tell ! What hast thou seen ? "

Lord God forgive us, beggars that we are ;
Flaunting the smart scholastic cap and gown,
Unconscious that we wear a leper's rags ;
Refusing to accept but what we know,
When we know nothing ; gathering up the chaff
And casting to the winds the precious grain
Garnered from age to age to feed the soul.
Give us if but the smallest crumb that falls
From Thy full table, rather than these husks.
Teach us anew the alphabet of Faith !

AGATHOS.

AGATHOS:

A VISION.

IN HOLY MEMORY OF JOHN KEBLE.

FRIEND of the gentle heart,
I watch the fluttering skylark soar and sing
From Fairford's grassy meads, till song and wing
    Are of the heavens a part.

Beneath these chestnut-trees
Along the Coln, I see the swallows skim
And catch the distant sheepfold's tinkling hymn
    Borne on the October breeze.

The tranquil sky is bright
With snowy clouds, as if Saint Michael's guard
In holy bivouac kept their watch and ward
    Till All-Saints' perfect light.

Beside this rustic gate
I linger lovingly, and, silent, dream
Of a fair boy, to whom each tree and stream
    Was friend and guide and mate;

    To whom the mountain pine,
The hoary crag, the darkling woodland spring,
The ant, the bee, the simplest sylvan thing
    Spake with a voice divine;

    Whose clear subjective eye
Read *Benedicite* in the stars of heaven;
Traced the gold legend on the clouds of even,
    And from the dappled sky

    Caught the rare power to string
His harp to those high themes that link his name
With Ambrose and Augustine in a fame
    The Church shall always sing.

    Through green Saint Aldwyn's lanes
I reach the gray church-porch. With reverent feet
I enter, my Confession to repeat
    Before these chancel-panes.

Softly the prismic rays
Flood the pure altar linen and outpour
Their rich libation over arch and floor,
　　While choir and organ raise

The blessed Virgin's hymn;
And as the tide of swelling harmonies
Surges through nave and transept, my rapt eyes
　　With happy tears are dim.

Now—joy of all most sweet—
I see a pilgrim in his surplice stand
Beside Saint Aldwyn's priest, with lifted hand
　　One *Credo* to repeat;

And when in solemn awe
America with England chants the prayer
Lighten our darkness, comes before me there
　　The ladder Jacob saw.

Lighten our darkness, Lord!
Night comes apace—grant us Thy way to know
Undoubting! *Nunc dimittis.* Calm I go,
　　According to Thy word.

O'er Hampshire's billowy down
Rise the dark roofs of Winchester.   How fleet
My thoughts, as I approach, with gladsome feet,
    The grand historic town!

In the cathedral old,
I drink the beauty of the lights and glooms,
The chantries rare, the quaint and storied tombs,
    The stains of green and gold.

Yon clustered towers beguile
My wandering gaze.   I pass the gates, and walk
Where Herbert, Donne, and Walton, used to talk
    In cloister, stall, and aisle.

The morning, rosy-red,
Flushes this wall.   I read the name of Ken
Scrawled in a schoolboy's autograph, and then
    With lifted heart and head

I sing, *Awake my soul!*
My spirit mounting on exultant wing
To those white cloisters where the sainted sing
    Safe in their sheltered goal.

But here I may not stay.
There is one shrine, beloved o'er all the rest,
Where, ere the swift ship bear me to the West,
    I long to kneel and pray.

How soft this noontide light
On Hursley's quiet vicarage; how clear
These English skies that saw " The Christian Year "
    Complete its chaplet bright!

Fair is this room, and grave
With sober beauty, roof and tree; yet keep
My eager feet no more, but let me weep
    Where yonder grasses wave.

I do not kneel—I cling
Close to this lowly grave. These All-Saints skies
Tell me this sod is precious in the eyes
    Of Christ our risen King.

Then, Jesu, may not we
Love this dear dust which Thou hast said shall be
Made glorious in that day when land and sea
    Give back Thine own to Thee?

O genius clear and fine,
Sounding with subtle skill the cosmic deeps
Of mathematic lore, where Wisdom keeps
 Her secrets most divine; .

O spirit unbeguiled,
Neighbour-familiar with the seers of old,
Bard, singer, artifex, and prophet bold,
 Yet lowly as a child;

O honey-laden lips,
O patient faithful heart, O thoughtful brow,
O starry eyes, hid from our fondness now,
 In death's supreme eclipse!

I lay my tear-stained face
On this green turf—I break, with reverent touch,
This sprig of sage—how little, yet how much!—
 I turn to leave the place—

And lo! the silver sound
Of sweet St. Mary's bell has called me back
From hallowed contemplation's storied track;
 I tread no English ground,

I breathe no English air ;
But sit alone beneath these tropic skies,
Holding upon my palm, with misty eyes,
    A lock of Keble's hair.

And thou—what shall I say
To thee for this thy gift ? My soul's deep springs
Are strangely stirred, as 'midst my precious things
    These silver strands I lay.

Rare jewels for the gay,
Garter and rose for victors; but to me
How dearer far, from friends across the sea
    This faded tress of gray !

Sun of my soul ! The East
Drapes her red vestments with the spotless snow
Of morning's fair cloud-altar. Let us go
    To our communion-feast ;

And kneeling here alone
Where Christ's dear saints have knelt with us of yore,
Where still they kneel, though gliding feet no more
    We hear, nor gentle tone—
7

Pray that to us be given
Grace so to follow in their path of light,
That with them we may sing, in robes of white,
Sun of my soul, in heaven.

LA BELLE JUSTINE.

On field and wood and sea the noontide sun
Unpitying pours his batteries of fire.
Along the low horizon, dusky clouds
Fade swift, a phantom army, while afar
Looms a red haze, like smoke from pillaged homes
Burnt and beleaguered.   From the bay-trees tall
The long, weird moss, in shadowy, gray festoons
Droops prone, as in a picture.   Motionless
The feathery weesatch [1] spreads its tent of lace;
Like an enchantress, o'er the chaparral dense
The love-vine [2] weaves her net, and climbing far
From branch to branch her amber necklace flings.
Past the dark forest's thick and tangled fringe

[1] A lovely tree of the acacia family.

[2] A parasite of the Southern woods, the stems and flowers—there are
no leaves—of a pale amber color. Its seeds take root in the ground, but
the creeper soon fastens on some tree or shrub, and, coiling itself there,
the root dies and the plant flourishes more vigorously than ever, in the air.

Of shrub and clambering brier, the dusty road
Writhes like a serpent in the glaring heat,
And all is silent, save, in some lagoon,
The gray crane's hollow trumpet.

                              In her arms
Clasping a sleeping child, a wanderer treads
The hot and dusty highway.   Hour by hour
Her slender feet have trudged since yesterday;
Those tender feet, so lately resting soft
On velvet cushions; careless now of toil
Or heat or fear or danger, so they fly
From that dread city where carousing mirth
Mocks at disease and death; where gasping groans
Gurgle through parching throats that vainly beg
For water, in the festering dens of want;
While reckless revellers in saloon and hall
Scatter life's priceless jewel-hours away
Like children tossing pearls into the sea
Unmindful of their worth.

                              She has come forth,
But not in fear of pestilence, though the Plague
Stalks with his noiseless shoon from door to door.
Her hand was readiest the hot brow to bathe,

The feverish lip to cool ; her voice to breathe
Kind solace in the failing ear, beneath
Death's hammer deadening.   But there is a blight
More fearful than the fever of the South ;
A wilder sorrow than the helpless cries
Of motherless children sobbing in the night ;
A look more terrible than the spirit's gaze
Striving to pierce the death-film : The gray mould
That settles on the wrung heart's tattered robes ;
The moan of faith slow perishing amidst
The trampled flowers of promise ; and the look
Stony and cold, which, like a jagged flint,
Is struck into the soul from eyes that once
Sent forth the silver shafts of love alone ;
From these she flies, with trembling, pallid lips
Stammering a prayer for peace.   Oh for one voice,
One faithful voice of breeze or bird or stream,
To breathe its benediction !

                      Dim, afar,
On the horizon's dusky line, arise
The roofs and chimneys of her native town.
She sees Saint Saviour's dark asylum towers
Midst gardens belted by a crystal stream,
Where witless, woeful creatures restless flit

Or aimless stand beneath the embowering trees.
O changing years! whose flowers have bloomed but
　　twice,
But twice, since from yon belfry on the height
Pealed the glad marriage-bell; since, bright with hope,
A joyous escort led a joyous bride
Along the hill-side path, while, crowding close
Behind Saint Saviour's hedge, the wretched ones
Smiled on her, tendering thus their broken thanks
For many a gentle kindness at her hands.
The sunlight glancing from the chapel spire
Pierces her like a sword; she hurries on;
When, near the asylum grounds, a haggard face
Rivets her flying feet.　Beside the gate,
A jabbering figure in a faded gown,
Wearing upon her head a threadbare scarf
Fantastic wound, sits rocking to and fro,
And muttering in the sun, while through her long
And bony fingers busily she sifts
The ashen dust, repeating now and then,
With low and senseless laughter, the refrain
La Belle Justine.

　　　　　　　Her own, her household name,
Woven into rhymes of compliment and set

To the soft measure of a Tuscan tune;
La Belle Justine, a lay of love and faith
And twilight peace and calm, babbled and mouthed
By this poor drivelling thing! She knows it now,
The story rumour whispered long ago
Of a young girl who dwelt in peace beside
The pebble-paved Amite, the one sole ray
Brightening a widowed mother's humble cot,
Till a light summer traveller who had come
From the gay capital to drink the strength
Of the great pine-woods and the simple health
Of sylvan people, set her innocent pulse
Aflame with songs of passion; and with gifts—
Quaint ear-rings wrought of beaten Mexican gold,
Chains for her throat and amber for her hair—
Used all a robber's wiles to steal from her
The priceless pearl of honour. She had wept
Over this story of a bad man's craft,
Nor dreamed 'twas he who sung, in after-years,
La Belle Justine beside her own low porch,
And won her from her home, a lawful bride,
Only to find in his, though princely fair,
A Tophet of despair.

     Transfixed she stands
Beside the lone dementate; but again

With quickened pace she hurries on her way.
Why should she linger? Balm nor aconite
Can soothe that fatal sickness, nor kind words
Awaken in that soul's discordant strings
One vibrant echo. So, while tremors chill
Like serpents creep along her tottering limbs,
She turns aside into a lonely path
And with a shudder lifts her startled face
In thankfulness to heaven that she has still
The light of reason left.

                    The breathless night
Broods like an incantation as she sits
Beside the deep, dark river. Sobbing low
Beneath the sombre arches of the bridge,
The waters moan, as if they felt the shame
That stays her feet from crossing; bitter shame,
The bitterer for her innocence! Yonder lies
The home which, in her dreary wanderings,
Drew, like a magnet, her wild feet at first,
Then changed into a terror, as she neared
Its peaceful quiet; so we writhe and shrink
When Memory on the tablets of the soul
Electrotypes her contrasts.

To the sky
Again she turns bewildered.   In the south
The advancing Archer draws his burnished bow,
Crafty and silent; glittering Scorpio coils
Beside the crouching Wolf; while, fold on fold,
Through the star-meadows blossoming with light
Trails the huge Serpent.   Must the very heavens
Scoff at her wretchedness with symbols dire,
And mock her with suggestions?

Closer still
She clasps her babe, and shuddering sees the night
Come darkening down; when lo! the child awakes
Transfigured, and with smile and prattle looks
Up to the brightening sky.   Her tearless eyes
Instinctive follow his.   High overhead
Vibrates the golden Lyre; on soaring wings
The Eagle bears Antinöus; through the boughs
Of the dark orange-trees the rising moon
Shows her bright shield, while o'er the waters dark
Shine the soft evening lamps, and flute-like floats
A woman's silvery treble, singing sweet,
" Keep us, O King of kings ! "

                              The compline bell
Rings from Saint Saviour's tower.   Her baby sleeps
Safe nestled in the old familiar room ;
And resting on her mother's heart, Justine
Hears the brown oriole twittering to the moon
Beneath the green veranda's bamboo shade ;
She sees the white mists stealing from the sea,
While round the dagger-trees the fire-flies gleam
And o'er the dewy terrace, incense-like,
Sweet garden scents arise.

                              O King of kings !
Inscrutable ! whose hand alike doth guide
Beetle and bird, alike doth trim the lamps
Of Lyra and the glow-worm, bid the night
Teach her its blessed lesson : That each leaf
And shrub and flower that trembles in the air,
Each cloud and star and insect silver-winged,
Unto the sorrowing and blighted breathes
Its silent *pax vobiscum ;* and although
The crawling reptile treachery has left
Its slime upon the blossoms of her life,
And the sharp javelins of a destiny
Cruel and unrelenting have been thrust
Into her spirit, Thou hast power to give

Strength like the eagle's to her broken wing,
Till, taught in Nature's temple, she shall reach
The shining heights where mildews blight no more
And sorrow's wailing minor key is changed
To the full anthem of the seraphim.

SONGS OF THE AFFECTIONS.

From Harper's Magazine.   Copyright, 1890, by Harper & Brothers.

BRINGING IN THE BOAR'S HEAD.   *Page 7.*

BENNY:

A SOUTHERN CHRISTMAS BALLAD.

TO

BENNY, IN PARADISE,

THIS SIMPLE RHYME,

INSPIRED BY A LOVELINESS OF TEMPER WHICH RIPENED INTO

A CHARACTER TOO BEAUTIFUL FOR THIS WORLD,

IS INSCRIBED BY

HIS MOTHER.

BENNY.

I HAD told him Christmas morning,
    As he sat upon my knee
Holding fast his little stockings
    Stuffed as full as full could be,
And attentive listening to me
    With a face demure and mild,
That good Santa Claus, who filled them,
    Does not love a naughty child.

" But we'll be good, won't we, Moder ?"
    And from off my lap he slid,
Digging deep among the goodies
    In his crimson stockings hid,
While I turned me to my table
    Where a tempting goblet stood
Brimming high with dainty egg-nog
    Sent me by a neighbour good.
    8

"God bess Fader—God bess Moder—
  God bess Sister—" then a pause,
And the sweet young lips devoutly
  Murmured—"God bess Santa Caus!"

He is sleeping—brown and silken
  Lie the lashes long and meek
Like caressing, clinging shadows
  On his plump and peachy cheek;
And I bend above him, weeping
  Thankful tears, O Undefiled!
For a woman's crown of glory,
  For the blessing of a child.

"SANTA CAUS! COME DOWN DE CHIMNEY,
MAKE MY MODER 'HAVE HERSELF!"   *Page* 107.

A MOTHER'S PRAYER.

THEY sleep. Athwart my white
Moon-marbled casement, with her solemn mien
Silently watching o'er their rest serene,
  Gazes the star-eyed Night.

  My girl, elate or mild
By turns—as playful as a summer breeze
Or grave as night on starlit southern seas,
  Sedate, strange woman-child.

  My boy, my trembling star !
The whitest lamb in April's tenderest fold,
The bluest flower-bell in the shadiest wold
  His gentle emblems are.

  They are but two, and all
My lonely heart's arithmetic is done
When these are counted. High and holy One,
  O hear me while I call!

I ask not wealth nor fame
For these my jewels.   Diadem and wreath
Soothe not the aching brow that throbs beneath
Nor cool its fever-flame.

I ask not length of life
Nor earthly honours.   Weary are the ways
The gifted tread, unsafe the world's best praise,
And keen its strife.

I ask not that to me
Thou spare them, though they dearer, dearer be
Than rain to deserts, spring-flowers to the bee,
Or sunshine to the sea.

But kneeling at their feet,
While smiles, like summer light on shaded streams,
Are gleaming from their glad and sinless dreams,
I would my prayer repeat.

In that alluring land
The future, where, amidst green stately bowers
Ornate with proud and crimson-flushing flowers,
Pleasure with smooth white hand

Beckons the young away
From glen and hill-side to her banquet fair,
Sin, the grim she-wolf, coucheth in her lair,
Ready to seize her prey.

The bright and purpling bloom
Of night-shade and acanthus cannot hide
The charred and bleaching bones that are denied
Taper and chrism and tomb.

Lord, in this midnight hour,
I bring my lambs to Thee. Oh, by Thy ruth,
Thy mercy, save them from the envenomed tooth
And tempting poison-flower!

Thou crucified and crowned,
Keep us! We have no shield, no guide, but Thee!
Let sorrows come, let hope's last blossom be
By grief's dark deluge drowned;

But lead us by the hand,
Thou gentlest Guardian, till we rest beside
The still clear waters in the pastures wide
Of Thine unclouded Land!

SHADY-SIDE.[1]

SHADY-SIDE!
Where the liriodendrons stand
Every leaf an outstretched hand,
Every flower a golden chalice
Held aloft in Nature's palace
With bright nectar overrun
From the wine-vats of the sun ;
    More than all the world beside
    Do I love thee, Shady-Side!

    Shady-Side,
Where, through vistas green and wide,
Arrows from the sun's red quiver
Pierce the deep and silent river ;
Where the wan white lilies lean
Ghost-like 'neath the willows green,

[1] Written, and published in the *Memphis Enquirer*, May, 1857.

Hiding from the garish light,
Waiting till the lonely Night
Shall, with spectral fingers, trim
Star-lamps in the ether dim—
 More than all the world beside
 Do I love thee, Shady-Side!

 Shady-Side,
Where the maple-branches swing,
While the robins ride and sing;
Where beside a cottage-hearth
Crickets make their social mirth;
Where the cattle in the dell
Rest beside the cool deep well
 'Neath the hickory-trees;
 But 'tis not for these,
Bird and tree and lily-blossom
Leaning o'er the river's bosom,
 More than all the world beside
 That I love thee, Shady-Side!

 Shady-Side,
Where the bluest, clearest eyes
Looked their last upon the skies;
Where the rosiest, sweetest lips

Purpled in death's dark eclipse;
Where the softest dimpled hands
Stiffened in white muslin bands—
    Where my José died.
Summer flowers sprang up to meet him,
Summer birds sang loud to greet him;
Violets at his violet eyes
Looked in timid, glad surprise;
And the grosbeak, crimson-crested,
Eagle-eyed and golden-vested,
    Kingly troubadour
Bringing from far tropic seas
Strange, entrancing melodies,
    Perched beside the door;
Perched where bright mimosa-blooms
Crowded with their rosy plumes;
    And, while José played,
Poured between the rippling falls
Of his baby shouts and calls,
    Sweetest serenade.
But, one morn, his blue eyes, lifted
Skyward, saw the flowers that drifted
    Snow-white down heaven's esplanade;
Outstretched, beckoning baby-hands
Wooed him to those Summer-Lands,

While a sweeter strain he heard
Than the song of any bird;
So, with mild angelic features
Turned away from earthly creatures,
That clear summons following on
Through the valley dark and lone
    Went he to the sky,
As of old a holy child,
Hearing heavenly accents mild,
    Answered, *Here am I.*

    Shady-Side!
I have wandered far and wide;
Where the trailing arbutus blows
Close beside the northern snows;
Where the bright pomegranate-tree
Blushes by a southern sea;
Where Canopus through the dark
Skims the waves, a phantom bark;[1]
    But I come again
Where the lilies lean beside
Mississippi's solemn tide,

---

[1] Looking southward from Galveston Island, the star Canopus is distinctly seen, for a short time in winter, a few degrees above the surface of the Gulf waters. It is frequently mistaken for the light of a distant ship.

Mourning, by the river's shore,
Little feet that come no more;
And my silent tears are falling,
As I hear the robins calling
 All day long in vain.
Every blossom, every tree,
Whispers of the lost to me;
So, to one who loves me best
 I would earnest say—
When to my pale lips be prest
Death's cold cup of blessing, pray,
Dear one, lay my weary head
Down to rest beside my dead,
 Where, the livelong day,
Sight and sound from Shady-Side
Tell how José lived and died.

IN SUMMER.

              I sɪᴛ in my still room,
And gentle noises, music-fraught, steal through
My spacious window.   The soft morning wind
Rustles the oak-leaves, and the gay birds sing
Among the hickory-boughs.   The kine go forth
Contented lowing to the shady wood.
The generous wild-flowers ope their fragrant cups
Brimming with dew, and busy insects sip,
Humming, the delicate nectar.   All the earth
Rejoices in awakening, but I bow
My weary head, and blistering tear-drops blind
My sight from the fair picture.

                       I was wont
To hear, with humming bees and singing birds,
A voice whose tones were sweeter far to me
Than all earth's melodies.   First in early morn

The patter of his little dimpled feet
Along the gallery-floor, and his glad shout
Of merry glee as he his sister chased
With tiny whip upraised, or frolicked wild
Beside his baby-brother, filled my heart
With a deep, holy thankfulness and joy
That none but mothers know.

                            All gentle things
Were teachers and playfellows unto him.
In the glad spring-time he would sit for hours
Beneath the tulip-trees and watch the wren
Building her tiny nest, or try his skill
To mimic the quaint mocking-bird, whose song
Held his young spirit spellbound.   In the cart
Homely and rude, it was his highest pride
To ride far down into the hollows green
And gather berries to bring home to me;
And then, with earnest look, inquire if God
Had berries and a waggon in the sky?
Oh, well do I remember how he came
But a few days before that fever wild
Fell on him, and with sober sweetness asked,
" Mamma, when will God come? "   I little dreamed,
As gently, with my heart hushed low in prayer,

I told him that we must be pure and good
If we would go to play on golden harps
With God's good angels—music filled his heart
With pathos deep and strange—I little dreamed
The radiant convoy would descend so soon
From their bright dwelling-place to bear him back.

Heart-broken, and with wild and aching brain,
I watched his rounded limbs attenuate grow
Through those long days of anguish. I beheld
The strange, bright wandering of his large blue eyes,
And heard his sweet voice murmuring low, as though
To unseen spirits. Up to God in prayer
My spirit went for strength—for strength to bear
This riving of the first bright golden link
From out my chain of gems; this sudden snap
Of one sweet string from my life's chiming harp,
Erst in such perfect tune.

                Those starry eyes
Beaming with health a few brief days before,
Grew dimmer as the death-dew gathered thick
About his lips, and in low, tremulous tones
He sang, " O Lamb of God! " our evening hymn,
Its simple tune the first his baby-voice

Had learned to sing—and with a long, deep sigh,
He died.

        Three years ago, I pressed him close
To my proud, throbbing bosom, and my heart
Brimming with untold joy sent up its thanks
To the kind Giver, for my first-born son.
With my own hands I wrought his garments fair ;
Day after day I watched the brightening grace
Of his young intellect, the beauteous growth
Of his symmetric limbs ; and in the years
Of the glad future's clear and shining track
I saw him in his perfect manhood stand
My crown of crowns, my life's best blessing.   Now
With my own trembling hands I wrought his shroud
And dressed his lifeless body for the grave—
So different from his cushioned, cradled sleep
Upon a bed of down.   What wonder, then,
When the glad morning's many voices float
O'er the awakened earth, and singing winds
Chant through the casement, that I sit and weep
For the soft key-note hushed ?

                I see the wren
He watched in spring-time as she built her nest

Teaching her young ones now to try their wings
In the clear waves of air, and to my heart
It teaches a sweet lesson : that my child
On tireless pinions cleaves the cloudless air
Of an eternal heaven, untossed by storms,
Undarkened e'er by tempests, and secure
From the dread fowler's arrows.

                      Bleating herds
He used to follow to the wood's deep shade,
I see returning to the river's banks
To browse along its margin, and I think
Of my fair boy by the good Shepherd led
Beside still waters, or reclining safe
On His protecting bosom in the green
And everlasting pastures. Full of peace
The song they sing to me, these innocent things.
The Hand that guides them all, will lead me too,
Though rough the road, and stormy be the skies,
To the calm shelter of my child at last.

9

DOES HE LOVE ME?

PRETTY robin at my window,
 Welcoming the day
With thy loud and liquid piping,
 Read my riddle, pray.
I have conned it waking, sleeping,
 Vexed the more for aye.
Thou'rt a wizard, pretty robin—
 Does he love me—say?

Lady violet, blooming meekly
 By the brooklet free,
Bending low thy gentle forehead
 All its grace to see,
Turn thee from the wooing water,
 Whisper soft, I pray,
For the winds might hear my secret—
 Does he love me—say?

Star that through the silent night-tide
    Watchest over him,
Write it with thy golden pencil
    On my casement dim.
Thou art skilled in Love's sweet magic,
    Tell me then, I pray,
Now, so none but I may read it—
    Does he love me—say?

HESPERUS.

I CANNOT tell the spell that binds thine image
       Forever in my heart,
Nor why thy presence seems to my existence
       Its very, vital part.

But yesterday a weary-hearted stranger
       Chance-hindered in thy way,
To-day with thee through thought's wide realm a ranger,
       All sorrow chased away.

As the clear sunlight drives away the tempest,
       So from thy gentle face
The light of heavenly truth illumes my spirit
       With its celestial grace ;

Calming my billowy soul to holy quiet,
       Till from all else afar

I turn to thee, and grieve, when thou art absent,
    Like night without a star.

I read thy favourite books, and trembling linger
    Over each pencilled line,
Weeping glad tears to find at last one spirit
    With faith and dreams like mine;

Faith in humanity's divine perfection
    And dreams of that fair time
When God shall see in us His own reflection,
    Cleansed from all stain and grime.

I hear thy voice from this my lonely chamber
    Amidst the festive throng,
And my heart leaps, as fountains cavern-hidden
    Leap to the wood-bird's song.

Thy quick, light foot-fall breaks the twilight stillness,
    My pain is all beguiled;
I meet thy gaze, electrical and tender,
    And am again a child.

Strangely my soul is hourly drawing toward thee,
    Patient of toil or care,

If, daily duty done, thou sit beside me
    In the calm evening air;

In the calm evening, when from earthly fetters
    My spirit finds release,
And rests beneath the wings of that fair angel
    Whose gentle name is Peace.

I cannot tell the spell that binds thine image
    Forever in my heart;
I only know thou art to my existence
    Its very, vital part.

ON THE BRIDGE.

(From Chateaubriand.)

'Tis midnight, and you sleep;
You sleep, and I—I am about to die!
What do I say?   Perhaps you watch and weep—
For whom?   Hell's friendlier tortures I will try.

To-morrow, when upon your lover's arm
Satiate with joy in search of change you go,
Lean for a moment from the bridge, and see
    How calm these waters flow.

ABSENT.

Why do I sing no more? The leaping fountains
   That laugh in glee when Summer paints the flowers,
Perish and die when with her glorious beauty
   She wanders southward to serener bowers.

Why do I sing no more? The wild-bird warbling
   Beneath the splendid midnight skies of June,
Hushes her love-song, when their starry glory
   Is blinded by the work-day glare of noon.

Why do I sing no more? The evening zephyr
   That plays with unseen fingers on the air,
Filling the forest with his witching story
   Of passion for the wild-rose listening there—

Sinks into silence when the grim November
   Blasts the fair blossom on her royal stem;

Or wailing wild among the leafless branches,
    Sings only Sorrow's broken requiem.

And I—the glad, low tones thy presence wakened,
    How can I tune them, now thou art away ?
As well invoke the spirit of the fountain
    When Winter rules where Spring was wont to play.

Through the still midnight, sitting at my window
    With face uplifted to the starry skies,
I gaze and gaze, until their silver glances
    Seem the calm splendour of thy radiant eyes;

And listening still, the while my tears are falling,
    To the soft cadence of the murmuring breeze,
I hear again thy low and tender whispers
    Floating beneath the dim and shadowy trees.

Give me again the blessing of thy presence—
    Give me the summer brightness of thine eyes,
And like the breeze, the bird, the leaping fountain,
    My soul in song will make its glad replies.

WAITING.

Waiting for health and strength ;
Counting each flickering pulse, each passing hour,
And sighing when my weary frame at length
    Sinks like a drooping flower.

Waiting for rest and peace ;
Rest from unravelling life's perplexing woof ;
Peace from the doubts that crouch like hidden foes
    And glare at me aloof.

Waiting for absent eyes,
Bright as the sunrise to the lonesome sea ;
Lovely as life to youth's expectant gaze,
    And dear, next heaven, to me.

Thou who didst watch and pray,
Quicken the pulse, bid doubt and weeping flee ;
Or if these must abide, still let me cry,
    Bring back the loved to me !

LEONIDAS.

Thou art not dead. Still, as I wait and listen,
  Comes the weird influence of thy radiant eyes,
And like a lone flower trembling to the night-wind
  My full heart thrills to hear thy low replies.

Thou art not dead. Still, in the sober twilight
  I sit with folded hands the while there comes
Thine image through the dim and flickering fire-light
  With saintly lustre lightening all the glooms.

Thou'rt with me always. When the watchful Mid-
    night
  Stands by my lonely window, crowned with stars,
Thy fingers, O adored and strange magician,
  Ope the dark dungeon that my spirit bars;

And taking in thine own my hands confiding,
  Beneath clear skies, beside clear shining streams

Where deathless voices soft and low are singing,
   The long night through we walk the world of dreams.

Day with its thousand cares around me presses;
   Night with its thousand memories shuts me in;
Life with its dangers and its dark distresses
   Threatens with sorrow or invites to sin;

But girding on anew my daily burthen,
   With patient spirit whence no doubts arise,
Remembering all thy tender, holy counsel
   I tread the way that leads me to the skies.

There where no frowning fortresses are builded,
   There, where no pilgrim feet are tired and torn,
We side by side will roam the heavens together
   Shod with the sandals by the immortal worn.

OCTODECIMA.

NORA, BORN IN JUNE.

CLEAR as her cloudless eyes
O'er cliff and glen and mountain's distant line
Undimmed by haze or mist, serenely shine
    The deep-blue summer skies.

    Fair as her sunny hopes,
The red rose bursts, the lilies white unfold,
The lotos lifts her chalice lined with gold,
    The star-flowers gem the slopes;

    And leaping waters play,
And gay winds pipe, and lark and linnet sing
As if each innocent and happy thing
    Would greet her natal day.

We bring her gentle gifts :
Bright blossoms with their loving type and token ;
Lichens and mosses ; curious crystals broken
　　From hoary cavern-rifts ;

Music of bard and seer ;
Legend and classic song, and ancient rhymes
Echoed from far phantasmal century chimes
　　To her enraptured ear ;

And I—I steal apart,
As scanning each with loving eyes she stands,
Her happy talk, like ripples over sands,
　　Cheering my thirsty heart.

O Saviour meek and mild !
Cradled, Thyself, upon a mother's knee,
I kiss Thy precious feet—I beg of Thee
　　All blessings for my child !

Thou Shadow of a Rock
Within a weary land !　Protect her life
From misery's desert heat, from sin's mad strife,
　　From sorrow's lightning-shock.

Love's fairest fruit and flower
Give unto her, and friendship's holiest ties;
That her existence, like these shining skies,
    May brighten every hour;

    Till, calm from morn to night,
Her day of earth a golden day may end
Fairest at setting, and forever blend
    With heaven's unfading light.

    Yet nay. Too much I ask,
And am too fearful. Only they attain
The evening welcome who, with patient pain,
    Fulfil the noonday task.

    Give to her spirit, then,
Thy rod and staff to walk the ways of life,
Thy shield and buckler to ward off the strife—
    Th' unholy strife of men.

    Each precious lesson point
That earth's meek creatures teach. On sea and land
Show how each high or lowly thing Thy hand
    With wisdom doth anoint.

Whether her lines be cast
In the choked city's panting thoroughfare,
Or 'midst the blessed woodland's treasures rare,
    Or by the ocean vast—

Oh, tune her subtle ear,
Pained by the discord of earth's warring notes,
To know the heavenly prophecy that floats
    From brook and bird-song clear;

Show to her serious eyes
The golden legend writ as in a book
Upon the steadfast mountain-tops that look
    Forever toward the skies;

And bid the ocean's roar
Tell her of harpers harping with their harps
Where shines the light of God, where sorrow warps
    The burthened soul no more.

So may her heart, replete
With holy courage, seek the victor's crown,
Till, all her journey done, she shall sit down
    With Mary at Thy feet.

A SEA-SHELL.

It tells, in its lonely sighs,
   In its *miserere* wild,
Its love for a far-off ocean-home,
   This exiled ocean-child.

I send it unto thee,
   Type of my own full heart,
That sings and sighs for its native land,
   Though doomed to dwell apart.

And when in thy listening ear
   Its plaintive music rings,
Let it tell of the love for thee and thine,
   That flows from my heart's deep springs.

10

SEA-WEEDS.

FRIEND of the thoughtful mind and gentle heart,
  Beneath the citron-tree—
Deep calling to my soul's profounder deep—
  I hear the Mexique Sea.

White through the night the spectral surf rides in,
  Along the spectral sands,
And all the air vibrates, as if from harps
  Touched by phantasmal hands.

Bright in the moon the red pomegranate-flowers
  Lean to the yucca's bells,
While with her chrism of dew sad Midnight fills
  The milk-white asphodels.

Watching all night—as I have done before—
  I count the stars that set,
Each writing on my soul some memory deep
  Of pleasure or regret;

Till, wild with heart-break, toward the east I turn,
  Waiting for dawn of day;
And chanting sea, and asphodel, and star,
  Are faded, all, away.

Only within my trembling hands I hold
  These bright weeds from the sea—
Flounce, feather, ribbon, crimson, green, and gold—
  Brought unto me by thee.

Fair bloom the flowers beneath these northern skies,
  Pure shine the stars by night,
And grandly sing the grand Atlantic waves
  In thunder-throated might:

Yet, as the sea-shell in her chambers keeps
  The murmur of the sea,
So the deep echoing memories of my home
  Will not depart from me.

Prone on the page they lie, these gentle things,
  As I have seen them cast
Like a drowned woman's hair along the sands
  When storms were overpast;

Prone, like the heart's affections, cast ashore
    In Sorrow's storm and blight.
Would they could die, like sea-weed!   Bear with me,
    But I must weep to-night.

Tell me, again, of summer fairer made
    By spring's precursing plough;
Of joyful reapers gathering tear-sown sheaves;
    Talk to me—will you?—now.

DRIED MOSSES.

CHILD of the sylvan hills,
I hear afar, down the rocky glen,
The song of the robin and the wren,
 The tinkle of glancing rills.

The oak-leaves overhead
Murmur like fond familiar lips,
While, stealing athwart their green eclipse,
 The sun, to my mossy bed

Comes like an alchemist,
Setting a gem in the daisy's hair
And crowning the timid violet fair
 With gold and amethyst.

The playful woodland air
Sings in mine ear like a happy child ;
Reddens my cheeks with his kisses wild,
 And tangles my loosened hair.

I see the squirrel leap
From the maple tall to the hickory-tree;
The spotted toad, renowned as he,
    Dives into the river deep;

While, on the reedy shore,
The oriole pipes, and the grosbeak proud
Eyes him askant; I laugh aloud,
    I am a child once more.

The peacock blows his horn
In the glen where the tall stone chimneys rise;
The black crow caws from the amber skies
    To the scarecrow in the corn.

I hear my mother sing
Her hymn by the open cottage-pane;
My brother whistles along the lane,
    To the partridge by the spring.

Two faces, heavenly fair,
In childish innocence look out
From the elder-thicket; my sisters shout;
    I bound to meet them there—

And bird and flowery land
Vanish away. I sit in tears
Holding these silent souvenirs,
    Dried mosses in my hand.

Along these sunny skies,
Cloudless and golden though they be,
I see no home-bird wander free,
    No cottage-chimney rise;

And with a yearning pain
I think of the bright Kentucky rill
That sings by the graves on the lonely hill,
    And the broken cottage-pane.

Though lovingly for me
Fresh fountains flow in stranger lands,
Fresh flowers are culled by stranger hands,
    Fresh fruits from friendship's tree—

That streamlet always sings
Of the sunken roof and the silent dead,
Of brambles that choke the violet's bed,
    Of childhood's perished springs.

Child of the sylvan height,
Whose gentle fingers culled for me
These fairy creatures of rock and tree,
　My thankful heart to-night

Goes to the pleasant South,
To that fair homestead where thy head
Nestles in peace on its downy bed;
　I kiss thy sweet young mouth;

And kneeling by thy side,
Soft, lest I break thy happy sleep,
Earnest, as flows yon river deep,
　I pray to Him who died:

Keep her, O Undefiled,
White as the lilies of the field;
From sorrow's blast her pure heart shield,
　From sin's sirocco wild.

Yet nay—each human way
Hath its dark passes.　Be her lamp;
Bid Thine archangel, Lord, encamp
　Around her, night and day:

So may she reach that land
Whither the loved are beckoning now,
The morning star upon her brow,
    The palm-branch in her hand.

A REQUIEM.

Leaves of the autumn-time,
Crimson and golden, opalesque and brown,
To this new grave-heap slowly rustling down,
    Come with your low, low chime,
And sing of her who, spring and summer past,
In her calm autumn sought that shore at last,
    Where there is no more rime.

Flowers of the autumn days,
Bright lingering roses, asters white as snow,
And purple violets on the winds that go
    Sighing their sad, sad lays,
Tell, with your sweet breath, how her spirit fair
Through life's declining, kept its fragrance rare
    Fresher amidst decays.

Birds of the autumn eves
Warbling your last song ere ye plume your wing
For milder climates, stay awhile and sing
    Where the lone willow grieves;
Tell of a nest, secure from storm and blast,
Where her white wing, the shadowy valley past,
    Rests under heavenly eaves.

Stars of the autumn night,
Crowned warders on the ramparts of the skies,
With your bright lances, holy mysteries
    Upon her gravestone write:
Tell of the new name given to the free
In that fair land beyond the silent sea,
    Where Christ is Lord and Light.

God of the wind and rain,
Seed-time and harvest, summer-time and sleet,
Stricken and woful, at Thy kingly feet
    We bow amidst our pain.
Help us to find her, where no falling leaf,
No parting bird, doth tell of death and grief,
    Where Thou alone dost reign!

CELESTINE.

Cellie, little Cellie!
  Underneath the skies.
There is not a bluebell
  Bluer than her eyes;
Not a lakelet margined
  By a daintier fringe
Than her long soft lashes
  With their chestnut tinge.

Cellie, little Cellie!
  Through the golden air
Not a sunbeam dances
  Sunnier than her hair;
Curling o'er her forehead,
  Or, in roguish grace,
Pulled by baby-fingers
  All across her face.

Cellie, little Cellie !
　Through the flowery South
Not a rose is blowing
　Rosier than her mouth ;
Pouting proud, the Princess !
　Laughing next, to show,
With her Grace's kindness,
　Four teeth in a row.

Cellie, little Cellie !
　Through the meadows sweet
Not a lambkin gambols
　Whiter than her feet ;
Dainty feet ! but palsied
　By a baleful spell
Since that fiery sickness
　Fiercely on her fell.

Cellie, little Cellie !
　How we watched and wept
While the fever-vulture
　To her vitals crept ;
Day by day beseeching
　That the risen King

Might vouchsafe to spare us
So beloved a thing !

Cellie !—Holy Saviour,
  Who from death's dark sea
Safely back hast brought her
  With us yet to be ;
By her baby patience
  Teach us lessons wise,
So Thou mayst receive us
  With her to the skies.

MY QUEEN.

J. E. K.

TALL is my queen ;
Lithe as the lily's graceful stem
And fair as her snow-white diadem,
 My Josephine.

Rare is my queen ;
My lotos, in her beauty's dower
Rivalling the rare Victoria flower,
 My Josephine.

Bright is my queen ;
The first bright star in the violet skies
Borrows its light from her violet eyes—
 My Josephine.

Gay is my queen ;
Birds that all day in the woods rejoice
Their gamut have caught from her warbling voice—
 My Josephine.

Kind is my queen;
Kind as the breeze at the noontide hour,
Kind as the dew to the fainting flower—
        My Josephine.

True is my queen;
Glad with the glad—Christ's word to keep—
And ready to weep with them that weep,
        My Josephine.

O silvery sheen
Of sky!   O birds, O lilies white,
Bless with your breath, your song, your light,
        My Josephine!

And ye, I ween
Dearest of all the Angelic Nine [1]
Seraphim, guard with your sleepless eyne
        My Josephine;

Till, pearl-serene,
She stand, heaven's light in her ransomed eyes,
At the jasper door of Paradise—
        My Josephine!

[1] "Les séraphins, ô Dieu, les esprits d'amour, qui sont les plus sublimes de tous les célestes escadrons, ceux que vous mettez le plus près de vous." —BOSSUET.

AN INVOCATION.

Beneath the tulip-tree,
  O spirit I adore,
Come while the evening shadows hide
  The clouds on yonder shore.
Above the waters dim,
  Night like a dark bird broods,
And, like a mourner, the low wind
  Sobs in the lonely woods.

From human love, my soul
  In silent sorrow turns;
And while Arcturus through the trees
  Like a red watch-fire burns,
With lifted face I cry
  Beneath the tulip-tree,
O spirit of the beautiful,
  Vouchsafe to dwell with me!

11

Love's flowers are very sweet,
　But blossom to decay;
Love's singing birds are gay and bright,
　Yet mocking-birds are they.
Twine with thy spirit-hands
　White amaranths for my head,
And sing thy deathless spirit-songs
　Around my midnight bed.

Bend low thy blessed eyes!
　They have no human ray
To mock me with the treacherous light
　That kindles to betray.
Oh, fold thy pinions white
　Around my weary heart,
And say, though human love forsake,
　Yet thou wilt ne'er depart.

Teach me the sacred lore
　That whispers in the trees;
That writes within the lily's cup
　Its strange, deep mysteries;
Lift to my thirsting lips
　The cup of Thought divine!

Its pure cool draught is sweeter far
  Than Love's red, flaming wine.

O rare and radiant guest,
  O spirit I adore,
While sombre evening shadows hide
  The clouds on yonder shore,
With lifted face I cry
  Beneath the tulip-tree,
Thou spirit of the beautiful,
  Forever dwell with me!

DOES ·HE REMEMBER ?

Does he remember ?   'Twas a golden summer,
  Summer among the proud, pine-crested hills,
Where the gay south wind, idle, playful hummer,
  Laughed, like a truant, with the garrulous rills.

Young vetches, clambering up the broad-leaved guelder,
  Peeped roguish, like the blue eyes of a child,
And 'neath the white tent of the blooming elder,
  Stood the wakerobin like an Arab wild.

Does he remember ?   Nature, holy teacher !
  Told through each living thing her lofty lore ;
But one voice only answered the beseecher
  That still had begged a benefaction more.

Kind words he spake—kind words, though never lov-
      ing—
  Which, o'er the billowy After, drear and blind,

Came softly back, like sea-gulls to the roving,
　Telling of all the green land left behind.

On her young forehead, sorrow-sore and throbbing,
　She wears the prickly Calvary-crown of fame ;
And praises follow all her steps, but sobbing
　　Through the blank night, she breathes one hoarded
　　　name,

Thinking how gladly she would yield her title
　To fame's ambrosial food and brilliant bays,
If she might feast her soul on one requital,
　The simple therf-bread of his earnest praise.

TWENTY-ONE.

Bright summer sun, to-day
Mount with thy glancing spears, a cohort proud,
O'er cliff and peak, and chase each threatening cloud,
    Each gathering mist, away.

Fair, fragrant summer flowers,
Lily and heliotrope and spicy fern,
Exhale your sweets from leaf and petalled urn
    Throughout the golden hours.

Thou deep-voiced western wind,
The stately arches of the forest fill
Till oak and elm to thine *andante* thrill
    As mind replies to mind.

Take up the song, and sing,
O summer birds, until the joyous strains
Ring through the hills, chant in the blooming plains,
    Gurgle in brook and spring.

And thou, O river deep,
Send from the shore thy message calm and plain,
As, bearing ship and shallop to the main,
    Thy mighty currents sweep.

Sing, while the golden gate
Swings open, and reveals the thronging hopes
Wingèd and crowned, that crowd the flowery slopes
    Of manhood's first estate.

Yet soft and low!   The door
Is closing, as ye sing, on childhood's meads;
The garrulous trump of youth's heroic deeds
    Is hushed forevermore;

And shining shapes that blaze
Like lodestars, with occasion wait, to lure
The dazzled soul o'er crag and fell and moor
    From wisdom's peaceful ways.

Tell him, O sunshine bright,
How clouds of lust and mists of evil thought
By chastity's white beams are brought to nought
    Through virtue's silent might.

Tell him, ye blossoms sweet,
How Charity divine her perfume rare
Exhales alike in pure or noxious air,
　　With holy love replete.

O brook and bird and spring,
Babble your simple sermon; say, Behold
Contentment better far than gems or gold
　　Or crown of sceptred king.

Tell him, thou deep-voiced wind,
How a brave, earnest spirit may awake
Responsive thought till distant cycles take
　　Their orbits from his mind;

And thou, O river wide,
Tell how a steady purpose gathers strength
From singleness of aim until at length
　　On its resistless tide

It bears both great and small
With equal, silent, comprehensive love
To that great sea whose calm no storm can move,
　　God's grace o'erarching all.

So may his spirit clear,
Untroubled by the scoff, the sneer, the sting
Of different creeds, find heaven a real thing,
  And walk with seraphs here.

  Thou great Triune! Thy sign
Is on his forehead; may he, manful, fight
Under Thy banner till upon his sight
  Fair Paradise shall shine;

  Till, crown and palm-branch won,
He shall before Thee stand without a fear,
Wearing the bright and morning star, and hear
  The Master say, *Well done!*

HINES.

HE sat on the humble door-step;
  His hand, which held a cup,
Looked like a crazy jackknife
  With long blades half closed up.
His thin limbs, all distorted,
  Were tangled in a gown,
And from his knotted shoulders
  A pinafore hung down.

Light-hearted, laughing children
  Were playing in the street,
And mock-birds in the live-oaks
  Made music wild and sweet.
He tried to join their chorus,
  But from his palsied tongue
Came only wordless discord,
  As if by witches sung.

The boys played ball and hop-scotch;
  They flew the paper kite,
And hallooed as its white wings
  Grew dark upon their sight.
All, all but poor Hines, shouted;
  Their fun was not for him,
For strange and ruthless fetters
  Enchained him mind and limb.

Through all his childish summers
  Beneath the cottage-eaves
Each morn his mother placed him,
  Where, shimmering through the leaves,
The sunshine like an angel
  Came down and kissed his head,
And vestal orange-blossoms
  Their incense round him shed.

He laughed to see the sunshine,
  He nodded to the trees;
But most of all, young children
  His idiot heart could please.
His thin blood, as he watched them,
  Would strangely flush his cheek,

And strangely would his sealed lips
    Essay their joy to speak.

Now whining he pursued them,
    With sad and witless stare,
As down the green lane flying
    Their laughter filled the air;
When, suddenly, they halted—
    " Poor Hines!" they said, and then
Back to the vine-clad cottage
    They quickly came again.

One bade the boy good-morrow;
    Another smoothed his hair;
Another filled with water
    The cup he offered there;
While one bright, blue-eyed urchin
    Stepped through the open door
And brought him out a toy-whip
    He could not reach before.

Then to their sports returning,
    They frolicked glad and free,
And poor Hines cracked his toy-whip
    And chattered in his glee;

While through the bowery lattice
  The morning sea-breeze sung,
And golden flecks of sunlight
  Lay all the leaves among.

O sweet, unconscious teachers!
  Ye prove that all of heaven
From our strange, sinful natures
  Has not been darkly riven ;
And that while little children
  Are left below the skies,
We may be safely guided
  To our lost Paradise.

ELISHA KENT KANE.

A BALLAD FOR MY CHILDREN.

LITTLE ones at my knee,
    The New-Year chimes ring sweet,
Silver-clear on the frosty air
    The blithe New-Year to greet.
But while the shouting world
    Its *vivat* sends to heaven,
List as I tell you a stirring tale
    Of buried Fifty-seven.

Once, when on glittering skates
    Blithe Januarius came,
Fleet as a reindeer leaving far
    His polar halls aflame,
Over the wintry hills,
    Beside the frozen streams,

One story strange he told by day,
    One tale by night in dreams.

Wherever an icicle hung,
    Wherever the snow lay white,
Wherever the gleaming boreal fires
    Lit up the winter night ;
On every icy rift,
    On every frosted pane,
With the busy skill of a weird fakir
    He wrote the name of Kane.

Kings on their jewelled thrones,
    Grave councillors of state
Trying, in diplomatic scales,
    The nations as by weight,
Each politic scheme forgot,
    Listened, with eyes grown bright,
As Winter whistled the epic grand
    Of that savage arctic fight.

He fought with sickness gaunt,
    He grappled with hunger fierce ;
He stifled, with firm, courageous words,
    Dark Mutiny's muttered curse ;

Seeking, 'midst crunching bergs
    Where the white bear growled alone,
Some token for her whose grief had roused
    The nations with its moan.

He fought with the drifting floes,
    He fought with the hummocks wild,
Looking to God, 'midst the trackless snows,
    With the heart of a little child ;
And bursting the silent gate
    To the land of dark and dole,
A trophied conqueror he returned
    With the secret of the pole.

A victor he came ; but the spears
    Of the monster he defied
Had pierced to the core of his brave young heart,
    And chilled its crimson tide ;
So, while the welcome home
    Still rang from mount and lea,
He voyaged out to that Unknown Land
    Where there is no more sea.

The Genoese, who first
    Made strange, adventurous way

Over the seas, had golden dreams
　　Of beautiful, far Cathay ;
And, fired with the magical show
　　Of blossoming grove and plain,
With an eager heart and a flashing eye
　　Sailed over the pathless main.

But he, our martyr brave,
　　There lay before his eye
Only a sullen, desolate waste
　　Where bones of dead men lie :
Wastes where no sound is heard
　　But the crash of the drifting ice,
No language writ, save, quaint and grim,
　　The frost-work's wild device.

Victors from battle-fields
　　Have come with banners gay,
But none with a braver heart than he
　　Whose story I tell you to-day.
Little ones at my knee,
　　Remember its lesson plain,
And keep in your hearts, as a precious thing,
　　The memory of Kane.

12

AMABARE ME.

When the white snow left the mountains,
When the spring unsealed the fountains,
When her eye the violet lifted
Where the autumn leaves had drifted
    'Neath the budding maple-tree,
        Amabare me.

Now the summer flowers are dying,
Now the summer streams are drying!
Yet I cry, though lone I linger
Where the autumn's wizard finger
    Burns along the maple-tree,
        Amabare me !

As the wild-bird, faint and dying,
Follows summer faithless flying,

So my heart, doubt's blank air beating
Broken-winged, is still repeating
   While it follows, follows thee,
     Amabare me.

Soon will Winter, gaunt and haggard,
Shroud a new grave, sodless, beggared;
Still, though not a flower be planted,
Not a requiem be chanted,
Not an eye with tears be laven,
On a gray stone will be graven
   'Neath the leafless maple-tree,
     Amabare me.

DREAMS.

Dreams of a summer land
Where rose and lotos open to the sun,
Where green *savane* and misty mountain stand
    By lordly valour won.

Dreams of the earnest-browed
And eagle-eyed, who late, with banners bright,
Rode forth in knightly errantry, to do
    Devoir for God and Right.

Shoulder to shoulder, see
The crowding columns file through pass and glen!
Hear the shrill bugle! list the turbulent drum
    Mustering the gallant men!

Resolute, year by year,
They keep at bay the cohorts of the world;
Hemmed in, yet trusting to the Lord of Hosts
    The Cross is still unfurled.

Patient, heroic, true—
Counting but tens where hundreds stood at first,
Dauntless for right, they dare the sabre's edge,
    The bomb-shell's deadly burst;

    While we, with hearts made brave
By their proud manhood, work and watch and pray
Till, conquering Fate, we'll greet with smiles and tears
    The conquering ranks of gray!

    O God of dreams and sleep!
Dreamless they sleep—'tis we, the sleepless, dream!
Defend us, while our vigil dark we keep,
    Which knows no morning beam!

    Bloom, gentle spring-tide flowers,
Sing, gentle winds, above each holy grave,
While we, the women of a desolate land,
    Weep for the true and brave!

BIRTHDAY–GIFTS.

FOR NORA.

PEARLS for my pearl;
White as the snow of her gentle breast,
Pure as the thoughts in her heart at rest—
Pearls for my pearl.

Flowers for my flower;
Lilies, fresh culled where the water flows;
Roses, to crown my one sole rose—
Flowers for my flower.

Birds for my bird;
To twitter and list, with eye askant,
Her rivalling voice in song or chant—
Birds for my bird.

God of the lone!
Left in my life's fair morning-tide
With but this child, I crouch beside
    Thy mercy's throne;

    And folding close
Her curly head on my broken heart,
Checking my sobs lest I make her start
    With my bitter woes,

    To Thee I cry!
Long is the way, and black and wide
Gathers the tempest.   Be our Guide,
    Thou Lord Most High—

    Till from the swirl
Of earth, secure in heaven's repose,
Angels bring roses for my rose,
    Pearls for my pearl!

COR UNUM, VIA UNA.

SAY this, beloved, of me,
When from my dead heart Southern roses spring
The whole year round where bee and mock-bird sing
    Their low sweet jubilee—

Say this: Through life's strange day
Of joy and sorrow, studying to be true,
With bleeding feet stern duty to pursue,
    She kept *one heart, one way.*

ADRIAN.

CHEERY as summer sunshine,
  Pure as the fresh-fall'n snow,
Fair as the early morning,
  Fleet as the forest roe;
Bright as the wild red roses
  Along the cliff's gray side,
Gay as the mountain streamlet,
  Was the lovely boy that died.

Summer on shining summer
  Lighting the pleasant skies,
Deepened the blue, calm beauty
  Of his frank and earnest eyes;
Spring after spring-time gathered
  With buds and blossoms wild,
Fresh wreaths of thought and feeling
  For the forehead of the child.

Adrian—just as noble
  In soul as name was he;
Regal in form and feature,
  And brave as truth can be;
Leader among his fellows
  At ball or hoop, or swing,
Tenderest with the weakest,
  And generous as a king.

Mother who sittest lonely
  Beside the vacant door,
Conning with tears in silence
  Each garment that he wore,
With troops of sainted playmates
  He breathes heaven's holy air,
Robed in the spotless raiment
  That Christ's dear children wear.

Father who listenest vainly
  For light and bounding feet
Gladdest in prompt obedience
  Thy simplest wish to meet,
With lifted face he waiteth
  On Christ the Master now,

Learning the lore of angels
  With earnest seraph-brow.

Warders along the ramparts
  That guard the flowery shore
Where wander all the little feet
  Earth's darkened homes deplore,
Blow with your silver trumpets
  And tell, in tones elate,
Another good and noble child
  Has passed the Heavenly Gate.

Thou who wast born of Mary,
  Child at a mother's knee,
Thou who didst not forget her
  On dreadful Calvary,
Bind up the broken-hearted,
  Their Perfect Comfort be,
And gently lead them to the lost,
  Beyond Death's icy sea.

THE SAINTED.

She has heard the solemn summons,
 She has listened to the swell
Of the lofty anthems ringing
 Where the white-robed spirits dwell;
And with sweet and willing courage
 She has girded her, and gone
Through the mystery and shadow
 Of the silent vale, alone.

Cordial greetings met her presence
 At the proudest mansion-door;
Blessings followed her light foot-fall
 From the humblest cottage-floor;
She was busy as the sunshine,
 She was gracious as the rain,
But the Master called her heavenward,
 And she might no more remain.

We shall miss her when a stranger
  Strikes the organ's stately keys;
When we bow, in deep adoring,
  At The Supper's mysteries;
But our grieved hearts will remember
  That with seraphs now she sings,
And that Christ has led her footsteps
  To imperishable springs.

Holy Father! who dost send us
  Angels sometimes from on high,
By their gentle lives to teach us
  How to live and how to die,
Give us grace her bright example
  So to follow, that at last
We may dwell with her forever
  When this life is overpast.

CHRISTIAN HYMNS.

ADVENT.

CLEAR as the silver call
Of Israel's trumpets on her holy days,
Beckoning her children from all walks and ways,
    The Church's accents fall.

With sweet and solemn sound,
Where winter's ice imprisons lake and stream,
Where tropic woods with fadeless summer gleam,
    They make their joyful round;

Joyful, and yet how grave!
Bidding us kneel with faces to the east,
And watch for Him, our Sacrifice and Priest,
    Who cometh strong to save.

As at a mother's feet
The children of one household sit to learn
Some sweet domestic lesson, each in turn
    His portion to repeat;

13

So, at this holy tide,
Calling us round her for exalted talk,
From each loved haunt, from each familiar walk
    She bids us turn aside—

And list, while she relates
The blessed story, old yet ever new,
Of Him, the Sun of Righteousness, the true,
    Whose dawn she celebrates.

Now the rapt prophets sing
Their anthems in each bowed and listening ear ;
Now the bold Baptist's clarion-voice we hear
    Down the glad centuries ring ;

Till, fired with joy, as they
Who spread their garments 'neath His precious feet,
With rapture we go forth our Lord to meet,
    Our glad hosannas pay.

Yet list ! Another note
Blends with the holy song our Mother sings,
And high above the harp's exultant strings,
    Clear, trumpet-like, doth float:

He comes to judge the world ;
To garner up His wheat, to purge His floor,
While into flames of fire forevermore
    The worthless chaff is hurled.

    Lord, we would put aside
The gauds and baubles of this mortal life,
Weak self-conceit, the foolish tools of strife,
    The tawdry garb of pride ;

    And pray, in Christ's dear name,
Thy grace to deck us in the robes of light,
That at His coming we may stand aright,
    And fear no sudden shame.

A CHRISTMAS CAROL.

FOR BABY.

RING, ring, cheerily ring,
Church-bells, loud and long ;
Ring as the happy children sing
The holy Christmas-song.
    Church-bells ring,
    Children sing,
Cheerily, merrily, ring and sing,
Hail, All-Hail, to Christ the King!

Sing, sing, merrily sing,
Little ones, one and all,
Sing to-day, of a Sinless King
Born in a stable-stall.
    Church-bells ring,
    Children sing,
Cheerily, merrily, ring and sing,
Hail, All-Hail, to Christ the King!

From Harper's Magazine.
Copyright, 1880, by Harper & Brothers.

"YE LADS AND LASSES, GO, FETCH IVY, HOLLY, MISTLETOE."

Page 5.

CHRISTUS RESURREXIT.

AN EASTER CAROL.

BIRD and beast and creeping thing,
  Trees and flowers and fountains,
Tell the plains of Christ the King,
  Thunder back, ye mountains!
This is Nature's jubilee,
  Let no discord vex it ;
Sing, O winds and waters free,
  Christus resurrexit !
Resurrexit non est hic,
  Christus resurrexit !

Wrestling in the wilderness,
  On the mountains praying,
Now He walks the wave to bless,
  Terror's tempest staying.

Soul, this is thy day of light,
  Let no doubt perplex it;
Lift thine eyes with rapture bright,
  Christus resurrexit !

Past, the garden's bloody sweat;
  Past, the bitter trial;
Jewish scoff and Gentile threat,
  Peter's dark denial;
Calvary's cross and spear are done,
  Death and hell perplexèd;
Angels rolled away the stone,
  Christus resurrexit !

Magdalen the tale hath proved,
  Magdalen, the winner;
Seven ways sinning, sevenfold loved
  Coming as a sinner.
Hear her voice Rabboni say—
  Now no sorrow checks it;
Sinner, sing with her to-day,
  Christus resurrexit !
Resurrexit non est hic,
  Christus resurrexit !

THE TOUCHING OF JESUS.

TRAVEL-WORN, among the brambles
   Grope I, sick and lone,
Vainly searching for the pathway
   All with thorns o'ergrown.
Holy angels! to the Healer
   Guide my trembling soul!
If I may but touch His garment,
   I shall be whole.

Pleasure's red and purple blossoms
   Wooed my foolish feet;
Busily the buds I gathered
   Filled with nectar sweet.
Far and farther on I wandered,
   Drinking deadly wine
From each deep and gaudy flower-cup
   As a draught divine.

Then—the noonday sun o'ertook me
  In a desert dread,
Where, 'midst faded wreaths of purple,
  Lay the unshriven dead;
Wild Remorse the only watcher
  By their graveless bed—
Stricken Rachel, still refusing
  To be comforted.

I have fled away affrighted,
  But each leprous vein
Carries up the hated venom
  To my reeling brain.
Still I see, though dim and distant,
  Christ the Nazarene;
Holy angels! lead me to Him!
  He can make me clean.

Through the clouds that throng about Him,
  Lowliest of all
Come I, with my spotted raiment
  At His feet to fall.
Holy angels, nearer, nearer
  Guide my starving soul!

If I may but touch His garment,
  I shall be whole.

Master, from the bitter apples
  Gilding pleasure's tree,
I am come, repentant, begging
  Bread and wine of Thee.
In the dust I crouch before Thee,
  Waiting my release—
Waiting till Thy tender mercy
  Bid me *Go in peace.*

MISERERE MEI.

HERE by the sounding sea,
  My knee, O God, I bend ;
And while the chanting waves to Thee
  Their solemn worship send,
In humble penitence I pray
That I be heard as well as they.

    They, that Thy holy hand
  Placed in the ocean palaces to dwell,
Dare never to transcend Thy right decree,
  But ever do Thine awful bidding well ;
Thundering amidst Thy storms, or, still and dumb,
Heeding the mandate, *Hither shall ye come.*

    And the glad voice they send
  Up to Thy throne beyond the vaulted skies,
Passes unchallenged through the jasper gates
  To blend with heaven's triumphant harmonies,

From Harper's Magazine.

Copyright, 1871, by Harper & Brothers.

" YE MAY NOT BRING HER FROM THAT ROCKY COAST,
THE STRANDED SHIP."

Page 15.

And certify that Nature's awful mirth
Proves Thou hast still a witness on the earth.

But I—I who have strayed
Far from the peaceful paths that lead to Thee,
Gathering the Sodom-fruit of earthly joy,
Forgetful that it grew by Sin's Dead Sea,
How will mine accents, trembling, low and grieved,
'Midst Nature's joyful anthems be received ?

I, whom Thy holy hand
Fashioned in Thine own image, and endowed
With Thine immortal spirit, unto gods
My feebleness erected, low have bowed ;
Laying on earthly altars fruits and flowers
Thou hadst demanded for Thy heavenly bowers.

O Father, all are gone.
Low in the dust my cherished idols lie ;
Lily and asphodel I should have kept
For Thee, amidst the bright wrecks droop and die.
Send rain and sunshine ! Bid my blossoms spring,
Peace-offerings which to Thee I yet may bring !

Teach me to heed each tone
Spoken by bird, and flower, and wind, and sea;
Teach my torn heart each wish and hope and joy
That stirs its depths, to consecrate to Thee;
So, when the sea and earth give up their dead,
Thy blessing, Lord, may rest upon my head.

VIA CRUCIS VIA LUCIS.

Dark Calvary's Cross! Thy holy, mystic sign,
  Traced with the sacred wave, our foreheads wear,
In solemn token that by grace divine
  With faithful courage we thy load must bear.

Dark Calvary's Crown! Thy thorns are sharp indeed,
  And weary temples throb beneath thy weight;
Yet we have vowed, albeit we faint and bleed,
  To hold thee better than our best estate.

Bright Calvary's Cross! Though abject be thy shame,
  Thy slender tree to Faith's uplifted eye
Transfigured stands, like Jacob's stair, aflame
  With shining shapes that lead us to the sky.

Bright Calvary's Crown, thou queen of diadems!
  Thy thorns are golden rays that blaze afar;
And lo! where blood-gouts were thine only gems,
  Shines, in their stead, the bright and morning star.

Fair Catholic Church, on land and sea unfold
 Thy standard blazoned with the Cross and Crown,
While we, the children of thy fostering fold,
 Exultant sing a Saviour's high renown.

Thou gentlest Jesu, Crucified and Crowned,
 Keep us, when pleasures smile, when sorrows frown;
So, bearing Calvary's cross, we may be found
 Worthy at last to wear bright Calvary's crown!

MEMORIA IN ÆTERNA.

Unto thy golden sands,
Bright tropic country of my love, once more
I come with exiled feet—how travel-sore!—
  From cold and distant lands.

Brightly the sun still shines;
'Midst living green, white blow the magnol-flowers;
The mocking-bird, throughout the circling hours,
  Sings in the clustering vines;

Fair as Damascus gleam
The city gardens in their opulence
Of rose and myrtle, flooding sight and sense;
  And hill and glen and stream

Glint in meridian light,
Or smile beneath the full and silvery moon,
As if no black eclipse could blot the noon,
  No tempest blight the night.

O gentlest friend !   We sit
Beneath these drooping elms ; the wind blows sweet
Among our Pæstum roses ; bright and fleet
    The finches sing and flit ;

    Yet wearily we turn
From their soft wooings to these hallowed grounds
Along whose silent, consecrated mounds
    The fires of sunset burn.

    What shall I say to thee
Of him, the patriot just ? how, stammering, tell
The virtues of that heart now resting well
    Beneath the myrtle-tree ?

    From blue Atlantic's bound
To the deep Bravo's mango-bordered shore,
His trumpet 'midst the battle's shifting roar
    Gave no uncertain sound ;

    But, firm and true and clear,
Cautioned the rash, inspirited the weak,
Rebuked the venal, nor forgot to speak
    Rare, noble words of cheer

To brave men fainting white
In hospital wards, to children in their tears,
To women strong in faith and strange to fears,
　　Toiling by day and night;

And when disaster dire
Furled the red cross whose light had dazed the world,
His voice was first to blunt the arrows hurled
　　By a flushed conqueror's ire.

And these—what shall I say
Of these, in battle-order side by side
Drawn up, to wait that time which shall decide
　　Where Right and Honour lay?

Dark day of overthrow,
Vulnus immedicabile ! for thee,
If in the future's Gilead there be
　　A balsam yet to grow,

Its healing shoot will spring
From holy lives laid down for freedom's sake,
From bold emprise whose clashing song shall make
　　The echoing ages ring;
　14

Its blessing will distil
From haunts made classic by heroic deeds,
From Shiloh's plain, from Chickamauga's reeds,
    From Malvern's bloody hill.

How proud these memories vast!
Giving us each a dignity and strength
Not born of earth.   They make us one, at length,
    With the dim, fabulous past.

Gathered from each red plain,
Brave, silent phalanx! kneeling by your graves
I hear the rush of those eternal waves
    Whose hymn has one refrain.

Ay—vanquished though we be—
O heart! beat rhythmic with my sorrow!—*ye*
Are of the Heraclidæ—mount and sea
    Attest your high degree.

Another classic age
Dawns from Potomac to the Mexique strand;
With Hector and Leonidas ye stand
    On history's blazoned page;

And from the sulphurous rim
Of black defeat, ye join the deathless shapes
Whose giant forms, like cloud-girt mountain-capes,
   Loom through the centuries dim.

Let bloated, vain Success
Be worshipped by the millions of To-day;
Righteous Defeat, uncrowned, hath silent sway
   To-morrow will confess.

Strike deep, though silently,
O Southern oaks, your roots in Southern ground,
And lift, O palm and laurel, victor-crowned,
   Your branches to the sky;

The river's heaving floods,
The mountain-tops, the steadfast stars shall say
Unto the cycling ages, *In that day,*
   Lo! there were demi-gods!

AT PARTING.

Farewell—shall it be farewell?
Farewell, said lightly when the careless part;
Farewell, said coldly by the estranged in heart,
    And serving but to tell
The empty dearth of cold Convention's shell—
    Nay, not farewell.

    Good-bye—shall it be good-bye?
Good-bye, low whispered amidst blinding tears;
Good-bye, presaging sad, long-parted years,
    Telling, with sob and sigh,
Of change or thwarted plan or broken tie—
    Nay, not good-bye!

    Good-night—shall it be good-night?
Good-night, which means to-morrow we may meet;
Good-night! I fain my foolish heart must cheat,
    Though morning's golden light

Shine on a lone ship leagues beyond thy sight,
    Yet still good-night.

    Yea, best beloved, good-night!
Good Night, best Night, with all thy fairest dreams,
Good Night, best Night, with all thy starriest beams,
    Watch by her pillow white,
And tell her all my love, thou gentlest Night!
    Good-night, good-night!

THE END.

www.ingramcontent.com/pod-product-compliance
Lightning Source LLC
Chambersburg PA
CBHW030104030726
47498CB00007B/2240